INVASION 2132

THE FALSE FLAG WAR | BOOK 2

RAYMUND EICH

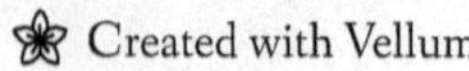 Created with Vellum

CHAPTER 1

7 JANUARY 2132

PREDAWN GAVE light but not color to the rolling hills on either side of the superhighway. The gray illumination made fields of crop stubble and little woods of leafless oaks look like photos of the region from two centuries past. Snow from the storm on New Year's Eve still clung to the ground on north-facing slopes where the low winter sun hadn't reached for a week. The rustle of sporadic traffic carried through the frigid air.

In his boxy sedan, Denis Leclerc leaned forward. He rubbed his hands in the flow of tepid air straining out of the vent under the bench seat. Yet another repair? Or finally time to scrap the old car and buy one more reliable?

Sybil would nod and agree. To pay for it, they could cut back this year's vacation planning. Forget Mauritius, Martinique, some tropical island with white sand beaches, where the service personnel and their robots all spoke French. Instead, a week on the shore, perhaps near Dunkirk.

Leclerc rubbed his hands again. He'd rather go someplace tropical, with the only chill coming from an iced cocktail in his hand, and his wearable computer declining incoming calls from his Humanist bosses or his Traditionalist collaborators at *Concordia* mission control. He could afford a repair on the sedan's heater. The unneeded luxury of a new car could wait.

A tractor-trailer rounded a bend on the oncoming side of the superhighway. Blue-white headlight beams splashed color across the sedan's cabin.

Leclerc squinted, not used to being on the road so early. And on a Monday. Coming in to deal with the weekend's snafu.

His hand groped inside a mesh pocket under the bench seat, near the vent. He leaned farther, until his fingers found the grommets holding the bottom of the pocket in place.

He leaned back and grimaced. Forgot to fill an insulated bottle with coffee before leaving his drafty old farmhouse. Forced to drink the charred swill coming out of the coffee machine in the break room? Bah, even most of the Americans knew it was garbage. Both Humanists and Traditionalists.

At least they had one piece of common ground.

The sedan slowed itself and turned on its right blinker. *Tick-tick* as the car took the exit ramp. Lights on the toll gantry above the lane blinked as he passed.

Two-lane country roads led Leclerc past villages and more fallow farmland. Between brightening twilight and the glow of his headlights, color tinged the world. Yellow-brown stubble of dead stalks waiting to be plowed under. Farmhouses showed red roofs.

Good country people. Most of them barely aware that data from the planet Alpha Centauri Bc, nicknamed Bravo Charlie until the science bureaucrats from both sides could compromise on an official name, flowed through Leclerc's facility not ten kilometers away.

None of them aware that *Concordia* had found an alien facility buried in Bravo Charlie's vast desert.

Officially, he too was unaware.

The ship's comms officers never spoke of intelligent life in their chatter on the line. None of the crew's personal messages to their friends and family mentioned aliens, though if one took careful note of the edits in the video, one might infer an omission. The gigabytes of data transmitted by the science teams only related to native lifeforms, from viroids and bacteriods to the pinnacle of local evolution, small, mute, and tool-less six-legged creatures. Their descendants might develop intelligence in a hundred million years.

But of intelligent aliens, Leclerc had no doubt. Remembered sunlight of a summer afternoon, streaming through tall mullioned windows, warmed him. A meeting more than a decade earlier, with the steady electric hum of thousands of cars bubbling up three storeys from the streets of Paris, and the broad oak conference table with legs carved into nymphs and dryads. Senior members of the Humanist Alliance's science agencies, most in from London or San Francisco; him from mission control; and Sandford, the coarse and vain British woman just appointed to be *Concordia*'s Humanist co-commander.

An abstract pattern faced Leclerc. A two-dimensional surface of solid white, crossed by straight black lines walling off a few rectangles of bold color, floated in the air over the center of the table. A virtual object, generated by his wearable computer from data shared by one of the science bureaucrats and projected into his vision through projectors like tiny warts stuck around each of his eye sockets. Everyone in the room saw the same pattern, oriented so each person saw it straight on.

Aggarwal, lean and swarthy, with bushy black eyebrows and a California accent, spoke. Despite his breezy demeanor, he held the power to make and break careers. "In your transmissions back to us, it's like, always use backdrops like this one."

Sandford peered down her narrow nose. "Abstract art?"

"Art in the style of Piet Mondrian reflects, you know, the

international and cosmopolitan values of the Humanist Alliance," Aggarwal said. Whether he was a true believer or simply deft at parroting official Humanist ideology, Leclerc couldn't tell.

After ten years of sporadic interactions with the man, he still couldn't tell.

Leclerc shivered as more recollections came.

Sandford tossed her head, sending a ripple down her white— pardon, *platinum blond*—hair. "Still bloody ugly. Doesn't mean a damn thing."

"That's why you're going to use it to send coded messages. Like, this one, with three red rectangles at the top? Use that if you find signs of intelligent life."

In her tuneful voice, still high despite her being of middle years, she said, "There's none on Four Freedoms." The official Humanist name for Bravo Charlie. Leclerc only called it that when he spoke to higher-ups like Aggarwal. Sandford, on the other hand, used it every chance she got.

"Like, we don't know that. There might be some today who aren't sending radio transmissions or lighting up cities at night or emitting infrared from industrial processes." A mechanical hum came from the ductwork and cool air spilled out of the vents.

Aggarwal raised his voice a touch. "Maybe they did, some time in the past. You know, they had high tech and lost it? Or maybe they died off and, like, left some high tech behind? Use this backdrop if you find any sign of intelligent life. Leclerc will pick it up and let us know."

Aggarwal caught him smoothing down his narrow brown mustache. Leclerc lowered his hand and nodded. "I will do that." The English words tasted like sand.

The science bureaucrat swung his brown-eyed gaze back to Sandford. "If you find aliens, tell that fool Varanathan that it's best to keep it out of the main data feed. If personnel at a relay station, or an amateur with a good setup in his backyard, pick up a transmission talking about aliens, it could cause social and cultural upheaval.

Better to tell senior personnel on Earth in person after you get back, so they can figure out how to release the news."

Sandford smiled. "Even better. I'd get Varanathan—" Her counterpart, *Concordia*'s co-commander from the Trad side. "—to believe keeping silent about it was his idea." She tossed her head enough to ripple her white hair. Still thinking she had the looks to twist a man around her finger. A woman her age had better tools than mere beauty to do that, if she cultivated them. Sandford clearly didn't.

A grin from Aggarwal. "That fool won't know what hit him. And when the ship gets back, like, neither will the Trad leadership."

Leclerc's brow crinkled. "I don't follow."

Aggarwal's bushy eyebrows jumped. "I'll bet a week on the beach at Santa Monica that the Trads aren't making this kind of contingency plan. They think God or Vishnu or Whatever made humankind in His or Her or Its own image."

Leclerc had his doubts, but kept them to himself.

Thus, a decade later, almost six months ago, across 4.37 light-years, the message had come. Sandford talked about innocuous personnel matters in front of a backdrop with three red rectangles high up. Late July last year, just in time to scramble Leclerc's family vacation plans to Rio and São Paulo, forcing him into frequent international travel for meetings with Aggarwal and his ilk.

Subsequent messages used other coded backdrops discussed in that long-ago meeting. The aliens who'd left the signs had died off. At least on Bravo Charlie. The knowledge had potential for immense benefit, to whichever of the Humanists or the Traditionalists could monopolize it.

Presumably it could also benefit all humankind, though Leclerc knew better than to bring that up with Aggarwal.

And immense benefit might mean immense risk.

Why had *Concordia* stopped transmitting two days before?

Pallid blue now tinged the eastern horizon. A tall mesh fence, topped with cameras and coils of concertina wire, came into view to the right of the two-lane road. Every fifty meters, a ground-level floodlight shone up at a sign bolted to the fence. *International Interstellar Exploration Agency*, in French, German, and English. *Unauthorized entry prohibited.*

Inside the fence, a path of crushed granite followed the perimeter. One of the younger workers jogged the path, in thermal leggings, long-sleeved sweat-wicking shirt, and a cap with flaps down over her ears. A six-wheeled robot in official colors trundled onto the frost-laden grass to yield the path to her.

The sedan slowed, then turned in at the main gate. He told the car to wind down the window as it stopped under a swooping metal canopy. Frigid air spilled in. Robotic arms reached through the open window and administered the usual procedures: retina scan, voice, and DNA taken from skin cells absorbed by the fingerprint scanner.

The guard came out of his hut. Thinning brown hair with gray at the temples and a belly lapping over the waistband of his navy blue trousers. A drip off the canopy splatted at his receding hairline.

As he approached, Leclerc's wearable popped up a virtual data panel on the guard. It hovered over the sedan's rear-facing front seats and gave the guard's name as Granger. Almost seven years with the agency, with two children, his youngest son aged fifteen and a skilled midfielder....

"Good morning, *M'sieur*," the guard said through the open window. His voice sounded like he'd been on his feet for most of a day, even though he'd been on duty only since six, with most of those two hours sitting in the hut. "A surprise to see you here so early."

"A leader is on duty twenty-four and seven." Leclerc pulled his overcoat closer to his body. "How is your son doing with the junior club?"

Granger gave a little bow. "Quite well, *M'sieur*. He has already been scouted by major clubs. Not just FC Metz, but internationally. Eintracht Frankfurt and Fulham. He will go far."

"We'll see him in the Champions League final one day, no doubt," Leclerc said. He crossed his legs and looked at his uppermost thigh, as if reviewing a virtual document projected there by his wearable. Feign an interest in your subordinate's lives, mildly encourage their unlikely dreams, but of course, don't let them unburden their hearts to you.

A *bong* sounded inside the guard hut. Granger glanced at some private virtual displayed to him above the roof of the sedan, then backed a step away. "The formalities are clear, *M'sieur*. Please enter."

Leclerc gave an idle wave. Through a subvocal command, picked up by muscle sensors on the sides of his throat, the window rolled up.

The gate lifted. The sedan went forward, along a winding asphalt lane flanked by spaced oaks. Their bare limbs looked brittle, as if a stray touch would shatter them. Five hundred meters on, the view opened up to the nearly empty parking lot, and mission control.

The building dated back God knew how far, to some era when architects pretended there was beauty in thick concrete, tiny windows, and lines that did not meet at right angles. For almost two centuries, it had always served some international purpose, for cooperating with Germans, Europeans, or Traditionalists.

IIEA took possession of it during the planning stage of the *Concordia* mission, now almost fifteen years ago. Yet the agency's presence there seemed ever temporary. The ugly, domineering design made mere human lives an afterthought, like insects living in the cracks of some alien artifact.

Such as the explorers on Bravo Charlie?

Leclerc sucked in a breath.

Such as *Concordia*?

Oblivious of his worries, his sedan found its spot nearest the front door. He climbed out and hurried along the footpath. The soles of his black leather lace-ups clacked louder than usual in the chill morning.

The front door seemed another afterthought, tucked into the bottom of a wall sharply angled to the path. Visitors had wandered for minutes along the front lawn trying to find it.

He repeated the security procedures at a kiosk, followed by stamping his feet waiting for the green light. Finally, he went in.

The cavernous lobby had warmer air, but little other comfort. He always thought of the First World War-era pillboxes and defensive works half-buried in the countryside around. One shell powerful enough could collapse the ceiling or smother the exit with tons of dirt. His footsteps on bare concrete echoed off the double-height white paneled walls. An image dominated one of them, and provided some relief from the austere and forlorn space.

A mural, an artist's rendition of *Concordia* orbiting Bravo Charlie, painted while the ship's specs underwent debate and before the planet had been mapped in detail. Only five pods ringed *Concordia*'s central spine, not six, and below, an archipelago of islands instead of a single supercontinent.

No matter. Minor features might be wrong, but the artist had captured the spirit of adventure and cooperation held forth as the mission's ideals.

Maybe something good for all humankind would come from it, after all.

Bright video monitors glowed close to the floor near the mural. An installation of a hundred and fifty video loops in a grid fifteen wide and ten high, one for each member of the *Concordia* mission, offering goodbyes and well-wishes recorded before their departure a decade past.

A chill ran over him, and not from the building's inefficient heating system. The ship and all its personnel, crew and scientists, Humanist and Traditionalist, should now be over halfway home.

If they had departed the Alpha Centauri system on time.

CHAPTER 2

7 JANUARY 2132

HE TRUDGED up a slightly curving stairway, wide metal treads and open risers. The treads flexed under each of his steps. He shucked his overcoat in his office and retrieving a ceramic cup, a souvenir of a mountain gorilla preserve in Rwanda, he stopped by the break room for what passed for coffee, then went down the hall to the command center.

Though as cavernous as the lobby, the command center always felt lively, as if a decade of the best and brightest working for a common goal had softened stiff walls and lines. As tall as the building's lobby, a mass of video displays filled the command center's front wall, opposite the door he took. He entered on the second level, onto a wide gantry ringing the room's other three sides.

His gaze always ran over the video wall when he came in, looking for anomalies. Easy to spot, this time. The largest display, in the center, always showed *Concordia*'s view of the planet below. Not now. Deep black, with yellow text in the foreground. *No signal. Retrying.*

Smaller screens, usually showing internal views from the ship's control room, or live data from operations on-planet at the official base camps, Glenn and Yang Stations, also turned up blank.

Normally, coming in on the gantry evoked happy times. The desks and sitting area tables up here, all geometric lines and golden-brown, lacquered wood, reminded him of the university library decades ago. But now, at the workstations set in back-to-back pairs, as many people played solitaire or browsed the web as processed back-logged data. At least the first time-wasters looked embarrassed when he approached, and the farther ones scrambled to cover their tracks. Which only gave themselves away.

At the head of the stairs, Leclerc looked down and paused.

Faces at the central station turned to him, fearful, angry, hopeful.

He descended the stairs, taking stock. The central station, shaped like the letter *U*, had eight screens and keyboards deployed around its inner arc, tucked under a wooden ledge running along the station's perimeter. Everyone called it the horseshoe.

A stuffed chimera, eagle head and lion body, drooped on the ledge, its iridescent eyes staring at the dark screen. Someone years ago called it the mission mascot and the tradition stuck. The curved end of the horseshoe pointed at the video wall, like an observation post peering forward, past the front lines of ignorance, an enemy to be pushed back a little further each day.

Today's enemy, though, looked to be dissension. Two of his people huddled together at the open end of the horseshoe. Lanky blond Evans, who must have every tanning salon within fifty kilome-ters on speed dial, and Wojniakowski—Woj to the vast majority of personnel on both sides who couldn't handle his tongue-twister of a Polish name—who really needed a more flattering haircut. Woj, the Humanist watch officer on the overnight shift, had technically gone off duty three minutes before. Evans would take over for first shift.

Normally they would talk, of course, during the shift change, but not with their backs turned to their Trad counterpart and their bodies blocking her in the horseshoe.

Yasmina Khan sat on a black mesh swivel chair as if rebar ran up her spine. Her brown eyes studied Leclerc from under a beige headscarf that complied with the letter of a law that her thickened lashes and artful eyeshadow denied in spirit. Her snug turtleneck sweater and tailored pants added to the effect.

She studied him, plainly trying to figure out which side he'd take.

Leclerc paused next to his people with his posture open to her. "*Bonjour*, good morning. Ms. Khan, you will get overtime pay because your relief is late?"

Her back remained stiff, but her eyes softened a touch. "Please suggest that to Hagerty."

Evans pivoted smoothly to face Leclerc. "Morning, chief," he said. He had a California accent, like Aggarwal, but less slangy. And Leclerc would much rather hear him speak English than his atrocious French. He angled his tanned face and pomaded sweep of blond hair toward the darkened main screen. "You see our problem."

Leclerc sipped his coffee and winced at the charred roast and the cloying one-note taste of artificial sweetener. "We lost contact as I got into my car on Friday?"

Woj spoke up, eager to please. "Not quite that late. Second shift. 1916 hours."

"Announced or unannounced?"

"Announced," Evans replied, "but with less than five minutes lead time."

"And *Concordia* comms estimated six hours," piped up Woj. He glanced to the side, to something projected into his vision by his wearable. "Not over sixty."

"Unusual." Leclerc sipped more coffee. The char and the artificial sweetener clashed on his taste buds, the worst of both worlds. He smiled despite the foul taste and said to Yasmina Khan, "Since you're the only one working right now, would you replay the downtime announcement from *Concordia*?"

She mashed her red lips together. "Mr. Leclerc, with respect, I ask that we wait till Hagerty and Broaddus arrive."

Evans' breezy expression masked a barbed comment. "They are running late, huh?"

Leclerc gestured toward glass walls under the stairway. A sitting area for breakout sessions and other informal conferencing. "Gentlemen, a word?"

Evans shook his head. "You remember protocol, chief? One authorized member from each side has to be in the horseshoe all the time."

Leclerc's gaze darted between the two men. He reached over and patted Woj on the shoulder. "You stay here. I will cover your overtime pay, be assured. Evans, with me."

The sitting area held chairs and couches made of steel, black leather, and straight lines. The cushions were thick enough under rump and back, at least. Serving as a coffee table, an art object dated back to the building's construction. A glass box containing at the bottom a chessboard in midgame. Brass and steel pieces made from the iron harvest, twisted fragments of shells and military matériel unearthed from the nearby battlefields. From the current position of the chess game, supposedly the best line of play for both white and black was a massive exchange of pieces. There would not be a winner, just one side would lose a bit less than the other.

Leclerc bade Evans sit. With a few finger swipes at the air, Leclerc turned the glass walls smoke-gray as seen from the outside. Green icons in the corner of his vision showed all the countermeasures against bugs and other eavesdropping techniques functioned fully.

He went in and shut the door. A twisting gesture locked it.

After setting down his coffee, he settled in a chair. Traces of steam rose from his cup like smoke from an explosion. "What's got you mad at Khan?"

A sullen toss of his head swung Evans' gaze up to Leclerc. The

Californian leaned forward. "The Trads are up to something. Here, I'll show you Connie's last transmission—"

"I'll watch it with Hagerty and Broaddus."

"They're in on it too." Evans flicked his hand toward the doors. "They're usually here by now. You know that."

"Perhaps they're running late from teleporting to *Concordia* to turn off its transmitter." Leclerc fixed Evans with a reproving gaze. "What could they do? Drop the relay from one of their ground stations to here? That might last for an hour, until our next station gets line-of-sight."

"Sure, chief. But they're up to something." Evans looked over Leclerc's shoulder, to one of the doors on the ground level. "Now they can tell us.... What the hell's she doing here?"

Leclerc twisted in his seat. He froze except for a sudden pounding of his heart.

Three people came into the main room, in a *V* formation. At the point, Hagerty, head of the Trad contingent at mission control for the past five years.

Five years? It seemed so, so much longer.

Strands of auburn hair failed to hide Hagerty's bald crown. Stubble covered his jaw. He wore a rumpled blue sweater and baggy khaki pants. Transparent video glasses instead of eye socket projectors, presumably because he thought it made him look distinguished.

Not with that combover.

Leclerc ran his fingers over his own head, bald above the tonsure of hair over his ears. Better to accept your fate gracefully than try to hide it and fail.

Hagerty looked at the video wall. A bright reflection shot across his glasses. Then at the horseshoe. Then at the opaque glass box, where it remained as his feet shuffled to a stop.

A word from the woman behind him, and Hagerty veered his path toward the glass box, walking a little faster. A ripple of raised heads and whispers flowed away from them to the personnel in the farthest corners of the room.

Of the people approaching, one Leclerc knew well. Broaddus, a tall African-American. A short haircut faceted his head, and a three-piece suit in chalk-stripe gray clad his long limbs. A gold clasp held down his bright orange tie. Voted best-dressed man at mission control three years running.

The other person Leclerc knew much more by reputation. Guo, a woman from one of the Chinese successor states. She looked harmless, with a floral-printed yellow dress and a pageboy haircut of glossy black curling toward her narrow chin. A silver chain held a small pendant, green jade and milky-white porcelain in a yin-yang symbol.

Leclerc knew she played some role in the Trad science bureaucracy comparable to Aggarwal's in his. She only showed up in times of crisis, and got as many nervous looks from the Traditionalists around the room as from Leclerc's people.

The three Trads approached. Leclerc swallowed down his misgivings at seeing Guo. He led the way out of the glass box, then waited and extended his hand as the Trads approached. Evans followed, a clouded expression troubling his California surfer looks.

Hagerty's video glasses partially concealed the bags under his eyes. They did not hide the sullen edge in the man's American voice. "You're here early, Dennis. Coming to fix the blame on my people?"

Leclerc broke off the handshake. He had to look up a couple of centimeters to meet Hagerty's eye, but neither that nor the Americanized pronunciation of his given name phased him. "I wanted to get to the bottom of this. Just like you, yes?"

"You watched the last transmission?"

"Ms. Khan asked me to wait for you and Broaddus." A nod to him, then Leclerc turned to the Chinese woman. "A pleasant surprise to see you again, Dr. Guo. I hope you didn't fly in from St. Petersburg just for this?"

The Russian city, jewel of the Baltic, with canals and summer months without full night. As equally off-limits to his family vacations as the city named after it in Florida.

Guo spoke English like it was a privilege to be allowed to. "It happens that before Christmas I scheduled a visit for this week."

Unease flickered across Hagerty's face. Confirming she lied.

And confirming the Trads believed *Concordia*'s loss of contact was not routine.

The bitter coffee turned sour in Leclerc's stomach. Should he have called in Aggarwal?

Too late now. Even by a private plane, two hours to come from Humanist headquarters in London. "Welcome. Shall we?" Leclerc extended his hand toward the horseshoe.

Inside the *U*, Evans and Broaddus took their seats as shift officers at the control boards. Hagerty and Leclerc stood shoulder to shoulder, each behind his own man. Near the exit, Woj and Khan leaned and peered to see what the current shift officers did at the boards, and what popped up on screen. A faint perfume scent came to Leclerc each time Khan leaned forward.

On the far side of Hagerty, Guo leaned one hip against the desktop's edge. She crossed her arms with a rustle of silk sleeves. Her dark eyes regarded the empty main screen as if she already knew its secrets.

Broaddus's fingers worked the control board. "Replaying main feed from Connie comms." He twisted in his seat. "How far back before transmission loss you want to go?"

"Start with a minute," Hagerty said, his voice muffled by his fingers tugging on the skin between his upper lip and nose. An uncommon gesture.

Guo said nothing, but her eyes, gimlet sharp, darted for just a moment at Hagerty.

Leclerc said, "We can look at more later. Proceed."

The main screen flickered to life. Someone on the gantry clapped, three or four times, before the time stamps in the corner showed receipt time was last Friday at 1915. Transmission date, 23 August 2127, in the reference frame of Earth. After time dilation from the relativistic speeds of the journey, on *Concordia*, the transmission date was 24 October 2125.

In a fish eye lens, *Concordia*'s comms station was the size of closet. A European closet, not the room-sized affairs Sybil swooned over when watching American or Australian interior design shows. Gray foam like egg crating covered the walls. Some sort of acoustic material to break up echoes. Adhesive stuck a few still photos and handwritten cards to the door in the background. Comms personnel's mementos of friends and family on Earth. The desk under the camera held a control panel, a microphone stand, and a lidded tumbler of coffee. All normal.

Except for the crewman filling up the screen.

CHAPTER 3

7 JANUARY 2132

THE FROZEN FRAME showed broad shoulders, wide cheekbones, a crewcut like a wheat field cut to uniform height by a laser. Kuzmich. A Russian, one of *Concordia*'s shift officers, one level below the co-commanders in the ship's hierarchy.

A Traditionalist.

Leclerc drew in a breath. He owed Evans an apology. "Kuzmich doesn't normally work comms."

Evans pointed to the stamp of *Concordia* subjective date and time, then twisted in his seat. "More than that. He doesn't normally work anywhere this shift."

Hagerty tugged at his upper lip again, then stopped and looked at his hand like it had done it of its own accord. "Everyone's cross-posted to two or three jobs. Varanathan and Sandford spend half their time shuffling schedules."

"Not Kuzmich's," Evans said.

Leclerc waved his hand for silence. "Play. Normal speed. Sound here only."

Broaddus worked the controls. On screen came, Kuzmich to life. His icy blue eyes angled to something presumably visible in a private virtual. His gruff voice came out of speakers mounted underneath the horseshoe's ledge.

"Big dish diagnostics look odd." Kuzmich raised a finger to swipe and pan virtual data. "System recommends maintenance protocol number three. Will implement. Waiting to clear outgoing science data buffers before taking offline."

Kuzmich eased back from the camera and waited, like a blond stone. Some Russian wrinkle in the training of national service conscripts, perhaps. A tough man to play poker against.

Broaddus popped up an overlay window. Incoming data rates synced with the time stamp on the big screen. Certainly looked like a burst of science data.

Kuzmich looked up and left at some virtual data, then bobbed his chin, a single slow nod. "Outgoing data buffers clear. Estimated time to renew contact, six hours. Going offline now. *Concordia* out." He worked the control panel. Buttons and switches sounded click, click, snap.

The main screen went black. Broaddus froze the error message in place.

Hagerty pulled his hand away from his upper lip. "Clearly *Concordia* ran into trouble implementing maintenance-three."

An EVA—extravehicular activity, colloquially, a spacewalk—to work on the main transmission antenna. "That seems the simplest explanation," Leclerc said. "Occam's razor, yes?"

Evans peered at a random spot on the ledge, with a distracted air showing he dealt with a virtual message.

Leclerc mashed his thin lips together. *You'd best be fielding a personal call.*

Evans spun his black mesh chair and gave Hagerty a *gotcha!* look. "Did Kuzmich start the shift at comms?"

"I know as much as you." Hagerty blinked. LEDs in the high ceiling glimmered on fresh sweat on his forehead. "Probably less. Khan?"

Yasmina shuffled forward a step. Her right shoulder, facing Guo, stiffened and hunched forward, twisting her upper body away from the Chinese woman. "Ferguson started the shift. Kuzmich came in to relieve him."

Leclerc sucked in a breath. Ferguson. From Great Britain.

A Humanist.

Expelled from the comms room in favor of a Trad.

Evans regarded Khan with heavy-lidded eyes. "When?"

"I don't have the exact time. I must check." Khan tapped and swiped the air. Her sweater sleeve clung to her toned arm. "1837."

"About forty minutes before *Concordia* stopped transmitting," Leclerc said. He shifted his weight toward Khan. "What grounds did Kuzmich give to relieve Ferguson?"

"Routine blood work came back from Medical," she said. "The physicians found numbers far out of range. Protocol demanded he go immediately for further testing."

"I'd like a look at Kuzmich's relief of Ferguson." Leclerc raised an eyebrow at Hagerty.

The taller American scowled. "What's that look for? You think I'd say *no*?"

Behind him, her gaze still on the dark screen, Guo made a faint *tsk*.

Hagerty stiffened for a moment. "Do it," he said to Broaddus.

The main screen jumped back. Ferguson had ruddy cheeks and bulging brown eyes. Other than possible thyroid issues, he looked hale and hearty. He pattered in the audio channel while he pushed packets of ship systems data out the big dish. Leclerc had a weak ear for his dense Scots accent. Something about jokingly asking for soccer highlights.

Leclerc cocked his head in thought. Ask to see the transcription in subtitles?

Subtitles that would block part of Ferguson's body language? No.

Onscreen, a light flashed on the comms console. Moments later, Ferguson said to the camera words that might have been, "Wait a tick, got a visitor."

Ferguson unlocked the door from his console. Kuzmich must have heard the lock disengage. He opened it and stood framed in the doorway.

Subtitles might block part of Kuzmich's body language, too.

Leclerc watched the two men. Kuzmich, stolid. A person of average build walking into him would bounce off. Ferguson worked through all the stages of bad news. A dismissive wave, crossed arms and legs, drooping shoulders. Kuzmich stayed calm through it all, except for the fingers of his right hand. Though he hid his hand in his pocket, his drumming fingers flexed the jumpsuit fabric.

Finally, Ferguson trudged to the door. Kuzmich said, "Is nothing," and a moment later, "I'm sure."

"Let 'em poke me again and get rest of shift off?" Ferguson lifted his chin and smiled. "Nothing to complain over."

Kuzmich raised his hand to stop Ferguson, then spoke over the Scot's shoulder to the camera. "Kuzmich, relieving Ferguson, comms, 1837."

Ferguson looked over his shoulder and gave the corresponding line, then left.

Kuzmich came all the way in and closed the door. And turned the knob for the manual lock before heading to the console.

"Stop there," Evans said.

The screen rolled on. Kuzmich took the only seat and faced the camera with his usual stony expression.

"What are you doing? Stop."

Broaddus made a warding-off gesture with one hand. "Easy, easy. Working on it." He lowered his hand to the controls. The video soon froze with Kuzmich caught in mid-blink.

Evans spun in his chair. "Hagerty, how do you explain all that?"

Hagerty stopped tugging his upper lip, then turned to Leclerc. "Dennis, you need to remind your people to use good manners."

Leclerc crossed his arms and gave Hagerty a jaundiced look. "I strive to uphold the mission's ideals by encouraging civility between both our sides. But don't use that to pretend we have no grounds for mistrust."

Voice loud and high, Hagerty said, "I don't follow←"

"Why did Kuzmich manually lock the comms room door? Ferguson hadn't done so. Why did *Concordia* Medical send Kuzmich to tell Ferguson he had to undergo more testing, rather than send a message directly? Something's quite suspect...."

Ice pooled in his gut. He hid the feeling behind a wry smile at Guo. Heart pounding but voice calm, he asked, "What coded messages has Varanathan sent you?"

She pretended the words were directed at Hagerty. Her gaze remained on Kuzmich's broad Slavic cheekbones.

Leclerc raised his voice. "Come now, Ms. Guo. We are both people of the world."

Guo turned at that. The curled-in ends of her hair bobbed with the motion. Her face lacked guile. "I don't know that figure of speech."

"You don't need to. Again, I ask, has Varanathan sent you coded messages?"

"Mr. Leclerc, we both know that mission protocol requires all messages to be transmitted in the clear. The Traditionalist Coalition has always abided by that protocol." She looked disappointed. "Has the Humanist Alliance done the same?"

Evans leaned forward in his seat, eyes scanning her like a radar beam. Woj stepped closer to Leclerc, closing ranks with his boss.

Leclerc chuckled. "You need not play this game. Yes, Sandford sends us coded messages. Just as Varanathan does to you."

A strangling gasp came from Evans. Woj widened stunned eyes at Leclerc.

Yes, yes, Alliance secrets, as if the Trads hadn't already guessed they existed. If not outright cracked the code. He ignored both his subordinates. His gaze stayed locked on Guo. A crinkle squeezed mirth from his eyes.

"How does Varanathan do it?" he asked. "Cricket references? Runs, outs, overs, unders? Or does he not actually read all those classic books he claims he does? Either one would suit him."

The expression on Guo's face matched the set of his own features. "I cannot confirm or deny that Varanathan sends us messages in secret codes. But you admit Sandford sends coded messages to you?"

Leclerc rolled his eyes and gave the air a backhand swat. "We know what *Concordia* found on the planet." Him and Evans, at least. The secret of the alien base had been denied even Woj and the other shift officers, let alone the rank and file working around the lofty chamber. "You know it too. We can keep it off the record, but we should at least acknowledge it among ourselves."

He looked up. Around the room, the dozen department heads and their aides stared at the horseshoe with curious eyes. Their gazes shied away from his like men scrambling for cover from incoming fire. Leclerc's voice boomed, echoing off the concrete walls. "Get to work, all of you!"

With the roll of chair wheels and a murmur of conversations, the workers bent their heads to their tasks. Not much to do in the silence coming from *Concordia*, and they would strain their ears toward the horseshoe soon enough. It bought him a few seconds, at least.

Leclerc turned back to Guo. A frown sent a single crease across her forehead. She spoke with the voice of innocence, while her lips curled up, gloating in some guilty knowledge.

"I do not know what *Concordia* found on the planet. You do? And did not share that with us?"

Gooseflesh crawled up his neck. She knew *Concordia* had found an alien legacy. And if that legacy looked powerful enough, she knew Varanathan would try to seize it for the Traditionalists alone. Just as Sandford would try for the Humanists.

His gaze darted to the main screen, to Kuzmich's image. And to the comms room door locked from the inside.

Coup and countercoup? A civil war in the corridors of the ship and in the exploration camps on the planet below? It would take little to damage the ship beyond repair, or destroy it utterly....

He shuddered. Damn Varanathan and Sandford both. Knowledge powerful enough to fight over would be powerful enough to bring all of Earth into a golden age.

And Guo would try to spin it in some game of power politics between London and St. Petersburg, Alliance and Coalition, Humanist and Traditionalist.

Leclerc willed vigor back into his voice. "We both have a guess what's happening on *Concordia*." He jabbed out his palm to cut off her next lie. "Neither of us will know the outcome until she recommences transmission." He put extra weight into his next words. "If ever."

Guo blinked at that. She knew the risks as well as he did, no matter how much she might deny it.

"We have nothing more to do but wait." Leclerc turned away from her. "Evans, Broaddus, the shift is yours. I'll leave you in peace. Assuming Hagerty and our guest will do the same."

Hagerty avoided his gaze.

Guo smiled sweetly. "A fair suggestion. We will leave the staff to do their jobs." Her expression clouded. "As you say, Leclerc, what happened on *Concordia* is out of our hands."

CHAPTER 4

7 JANUARY 2132

THE DISTORTED SQUARE of sunlight from the solitary window crept across the wall beside Leclerc's desk. He had one of the two largest offices in the building, with padded carpet laid in for his middle-aged feet and a dry bar boasting a two-bottle wine chiller.

Like so much else about the mission control building, he hated his office. The air circulation pooled all the heat around his desk. The door hid in an alcove. The LED panels in the ceiling glowed with too much blue. Full natural solar spectrum? Please.

In summer, he took breaks outside, at the picnic benches under the oak visible if you stood tiptoe at his office's recessed window. In winter, as today, he drank a yellow-green emulsion of vitamins D3 and K and rested his eyes on the distorted square of sunlight, while daydreaming of his family's August vacation. Hard to tell which tasted worse, the artificial banana flavor of the emulsion or the coffee from the break room.

By five in the afternoon, the square of sunlight slipped away, leaving only the blue tinge and an impending headache. From eyestrain, in part. Exacerbated by the ship's silence and his sparring with Guo in the horseshoe. Compounded by last week's department reports still to review and a summary still to write for senior Humanist officials in London and the tech directorates in Silicon Valley. After sending the summary upstairs, he would compose his thoughts for a private call to Aggarwal, where he would share what he'd learned in the past week about the alien discoveries.

Sybil made a running joke of his working late on Mondays. She would raise an eyebrow. *Another tryst with your mistress Uranie?* The muse of astronomy. Her voice would grow husky. *When she leaves you for a richer man, I will still be here.*

Leclerc looked at the virtual pile of paper in his inbox. Dwindled, but not empty. He sighed and reached for the next report. *Assessments of Humanist crew morale from personal messages home, cross-compared with psychology reports from on-board.*

The final swig of his vitamin emulsion. He shuddered. It tasted worse after warming to room temperature. He flipped open the virtual folder and read the summary on page 1, then started skimming. Annike Ingvarsson, the Humanist psych officer on *Concordia*, had fallen farther behind schedule in transmitting reports to Earth—

A knock on the door roused him. A break from this drudgery, but also an added delay before he could head home. He rubbed the bags under his eyes and said, "Enter."

The door creaked open. Evans came in and stopped at the corner of the alcove. His grim face clashed with his summery tan and thick blond hair. "Chief, we need to talk," he said. Noises of shuffling feet and breathing came from someone out of sight.

Leclerc waved him a few steps toward a sitting area, a round conference table of red-brown wood and four black ergonomic chairs. "I assumed you left hours ago."

Evans started forward. "Yeah, chief, about that...." He looked over his shoulder.

The person at the doorway came into view. Brownish skin and thick eyebrows, low and knitted despite a social smile exposing teeth like a picket fence. A navy blue suit cut to a lean frame. Aggarwal.

Leclerc felt punched in the gut. He labored inside to make light of the bureaucrat's visit. "Good evening. And a pleasant surprise. Safe travels from London?"

Aggarwal strode to the dry bar. He faced Leclerc and put his hands on his hips. Over his shoulder, he said, "Evans, get the door."

The other Californian stalked on slow steps to the alcove. The bolt snapped home like a rifle chambering its next round.

Leclerc rose, gut churning. "Care for a drink?"

"Scotch all around."

Foul stuff, flavored like the dirt used to filter it. Leclerc his thoughts behind a neutral expression. "I'll pour—"

"Evans, set us up three glasses."

Aggarwal shifted out of the way. Evans went to the dry bar with a grin on his face. The grin faded a little until he passed out of Leclerc's full view. Currying favor. His star rising.

Leclerc beckoned toward the round table. "Sit, please."

Aggarwal angled his head from side to side. "Sure." He rolled one of the chairs away from the table. He palmed the top of the backrest.

Evans set down a glass of dirt-brown liquid in front of him, then returned with two. He put Leclerc's glass down opposite Aggarwal.

Leclerc raised an eyebrow at Evans. The lanky Californian avoided his gaze.

Inwardly, Leclerc fumed. If you want to play the game of office politics, play it without apology. Don't act like an American and try to have it both ways, winning the war while claiming to feel bad about it.

The LED panels glared worse over his glass than anywhere else on the table. Leclerc sighed and took the hot seat. He took a sip and clamped down on his shudder. The other two men sat and faced him.

"Again, safe travels?" Leclerc asked. He expected a minute of chit-chat, about heavy London traffic getting to the airport, or the gloomy rural landscape between the airfield near Verdun and here.

Aggarwal spoke. "You're wondering why am I here?"

Leclerc blinked, once. "I'm not wondering at all." One more sip. "Evans went behind my back. Over my head?" Maybe Aggarwal would fire him on the spot, and he would never have to speak English again.

"Yeah." Aggarwal drew out the word. "But, like, why would he do that?"

"I said the thing everyone knows. Both Sandford and Varanathan send coded messages home about the alien presence on Four Freedoms." The hours spent working on reports to his superiors had primed him to call it by the Humanist name instead of *Bravo Charlie*.

Aggarwal squinted at him. "That's not what Evans told me. You admitted to Guo and the other Trads Sandford sends secret messages to us. Guo didn't say a damn thing about whether Varanathan sent his own secret messages to her." He took a long swig of his Scotch, then clunked the glass heavily on the red-brown table.

Leclerc gave Evans a cold smile. "All three of us know he does."

Evans studied the tabletop's wood grain. Aggarwal spoke. "No, we don't. It's like, they're Trads, you know?"

Evans kept his blond head down rather than agree with such a foolish statement.

Leclerc slid his mostly-full glass away from him, exposing more of himself to Aggarwal's gaze. "I took a risk to try extracting information from them."

"And failed. You know, you left me with a hell of a damn mess to clean up. The Trad secretariat has already delivered a note alerting us they're, you know, going to lodge a formal protest under the IIEA Treaty. A formal protest! I've got to answer to people high up in London for this. Yeah, we'll stall the Trads for a week or two, but we'll have to eventually turn over everything Sandford sent us, you know?" A hard edge surrounded Aggarwal's brown eyes.

Leclerc's hand on the tabletop wanted to curl into a fist. He willed it flat. "Which costs us nothing. Everything Sandford sent us, Varanathan sent them."

Aggarwal threw up his hands and scowled across the table. "God-dam, I keep telling you, they aren't smart enough to have set up coded messages. If Trads were smart, they'd be Humanists, you know?"

Blunt words wanted to come out of his mouth. Why not? Aggarwal's unexpected visit meant he was fired anyway. "Only fools underestimate their rivals."

The bureaucrat blinked. "The Traditionalists aren't our rivals. They are reactionaries clinging to the wrong side of history." He recited the lines by rote.

Leclerc switched angles of attack. "Even if the Trad leadership on Earth doesn't know what Sandford knows about the aliens, Varanathan does."

Aggarwal narrowed his eyes and leaned back. "So?"

"Sandford told us the aliens are not from Br—Four Freedoms, yes?"

"Yeah. And?"

Sweat dewed on Leclerc's bald crown. Was Aggarwal obtuse? Or did he just act that way to make his subordinates talk too much? "To get to the planet from their homeworld, they must have possessed technology at least as powerful as particle spin magnets and Bussard ramjets. At least."

"What's your point?"

"A powerful propulsion system can be used as a powerful weapon."

Aggarwal's eyes grew both dreamy and aggressive, like a man eyeing an exotic dancer writhing on a table in front of him. "Yeah. I see that. But it still doesn't justify you giving away our secrets."

Drying sweat turned Leclerc's scalp clammy. "Why did Kuzmich work his first comms shift in years? Relieving a Humanist? Locking the door from the inside? And then comms go down for 'routine maintenance' that lasts, what, three days too long? So far? Varanathan attempted a...." Leclerc groped for English words, but only a French phrase came to him. "A *coup de main*—"

Aggarwal grinned. "'Cooter mane?'"

Hand half-ringing his Scotch on the tabletop, gaze on a ripple of light in the dark brown liquid, Evans said, "A killing blow."

A nugget of tension broke apart in Leclerc's chest. Evans might play politics, but he was not a fool. "Precisely. Varanathan found some evidence of powerful alien technology and made a play for it."

Aggarwal scrunched up his nose. "Sandford would have made a play too."

"Whose man shut down comms from the ship?"

Aggarwal leaned back. He propped his left cheek on his fist, elbow planted on the arm of his chair. With his right hand he swirled whisky in his glass. "I see what you're saying."

Abruptly, he sat straight and drained the last of his Scotch in three swallows. He thumped the glass to the tabletop. "Which means you put us, like, even further behind the eight-ball. Goddam! I was going to ask for your resignation, and if you said no, *promote* you to head of the ground station on Diego Garcia. But now?"

A miserable fly speck of an island in the middle of the Indian Ocean, housing a radio antenna array and little else. No tropical cock-tails. No service personnel speaking French.

No families.

Leclerc drew in a breath, like a man expressing a final defiance before the firing squad blindfolds him. Do your worst—

A bright red police siren icon popped into his vision in the notif-ication area to his lower left. The siren sounded in his earbuds, a long rise and fall out of some old American cop show.

He turned his head, eyes wide, the thin ice under his career suddenly forgotten.

Code Red-2.

Anomalous data from the Alpha Centauri system. Not from *Concordia.*

Evans mirrored his gesture. "What the hell?" he muttered. "*Concordia* back online?"

"Like, what's going on?" asked Aggarwal.

Tunnel vision narrowed Leclerc's attention to the siren. "Something serious. Excuse me." He rose, drink forgotten, Aggarwal ignored. His tunnel vision widened enough to take in the alcove. Adrenaline turned his hand into a thick glove. He fumbled with the knob before finally gripping and turning it.

He strode down the concrete hallway, toward the entrance to the gantry. LED panels on motion sensors lit up for him. Over the blood rushing in his ears came the sound of loping footsteps trying to catch up.

Evans spoke in his terrible French. "Did they get comms back from *Concordia*, chief? No, the guys in the horseshoe wouldn't push this alert for that."

Still striding, Leclerc said over his shoulder, "Wait with Aggarwal and measure new drapes for my office. I'll take care of ops."

"Hey, chief...." Evans increased his pace and finally made it abreast of Leclerc. "What could trigger a Red-2?"

Leclerc ignored him. Evans hesitated and fell a step behind.

The doors to the gantry opened. Leclerc stalked toward the stairs. His gaze went to the main screen.

His feet slowed, shuffled, stopped.

The main screen compiled visible light and infrared data from arrays of satellites deployed around the Solar System, all watching the planet Bravo Charlie. Despite all the tricks of interferometry, 4.37 light-years blurred most details. Someone in the horseshoe could blend in detailed maps previously transmitted by *Concordia* with a few keystrokes, but no one had done so.

Normally, from only near-Earth observations, Leclerc could tell at a glance day from night, or whether the slowly-turning planet showed its hemisphere of supercontinent or its hemisphere of ocean. Enough color came through to show the supercontinent's three concentric bands of biomes, deep green along the coasts, yellowing further inland where fewer rain clouds could reach, turning to the central desert, red as Mars and almost as dry, five thousand kilometers from the ocean.

What the screen showed now was not normal.

Two-thirds of the supercontinent, off-center low and left. To the left of the terminator, the line between day and night, Alpha Centauri B tinged the landscape with its orange rays. Just after sunrise in the red desert.

Where a second sun glowed on the surface.

Small. Guessing the scale, a few kilometers wide. But shining bright enough to fully saturate the handful of pixels. A text box overlay gave the glowing point's temperature of 8133 K.

Leclerc descended the stairs. Conversation fragments drifted up to him.

"...volcanic eruption?"

"No, way too hot..."

The ones and tens digits ticked around. Now 8145 K. Either way, more than hot enough to melt rock. Hotter even than the photosphere of the planet's orange sun.

Conversations dried up. The faces of the evening shift watch officers turned to him. Tung, a slender man with a thick head of black hair, had risen as far as the Humanist hierarchy would allow for a native of the Chinese successor states. His Trad counterpart, Randolph, towered over Tung. An avuncular white man from the American South, white-haired and wrinkled, Randolph could dial his honeysuckle accent up or down at will.

As they stood in the center of the horseshoe, both watch officers looked at him like characters in a sports movie. Nervous rookies looking to the limping veteran for leadership, with all the day's politics and suspicions gone.

"One good thing comes of working late on Mondays. I'm still in the building." Leclerc put on a little smile. He entered the horseshoe with his gaze on the hotspot of light. "Can you tell me anything more than what's showing?"

Tung spoke. "It started about fifteen minutes ago." American English, barely accented, and with the tone a loyal dog would use if it could speak to its master. Common among the generation of young

Chinese who'd done everything they were supposed to, to overcome the genocidal hegemony of their forefathers, and still were denied the fair deal promised to them. "We're reviewing geology data for pre-indicators for volcanic activity. Nothing so far."

"I have my doubts we'll find anything," Randolph said. His words had only a whisper of a Southern American accent. "Connie doesn't have any personnel within two thousand miles, three thousand kilometers."

Leclerc put on a blank look. In one of Sandford's transmissions, she'd squeezed a stress ball of two colors, one hemisphere blue and the other green. Her fingernail had gouged out some of the foam near the middle of the green hemisphere. Site of the alien presence, and the third ground expedition that only a dozen people on Earth knew about.

On the Humanist side. Double that to get the real number.

If the green hemisphere in her stress ball were a map of Bravo Charlie's supercontinent, the gouge marked a spot not far from the zone of hellish light and heat.

Leclerc swallowed. The location could not be a coincidence. What had the third ground expedition stumbled upon? "Is *Concordia* safe?" he blurted, and regretted it.

"Still radio silence," said Tung. "Over seventy-two hours now. But we have reason to expect it is. Its projected orbit has it over the far side of the planet."

Randolph played up his accent by a notch. "Is there a reason Connie wouldn't be safe?"

Feigning ignorance to lure Leclerc into saying something he shouldn't. A ploy that worked well on others. Leclerc did not fall for it. "Could a volcanic eruption with that much energy propel small rocks into orbit?"

"I have to say, that seems unlikely...." Randolph turned his attention back to the screen. The light caught long hairs growing out his nostrils. "8148 K? If it were a volcanic eruption, maybe it could."

Footsteps, multiple sets, approached the back of the horseshoe. Leclerc's gaze remained on the hotspot. "If it is not a volcanic eruption, what else could it be?" he asked Tung and Randolph.

A soft female voice sounded, with an accent thicker than Tung's. "I hoped you could tell me."

CHAPTER 5

7 JANUARY 2132

Leclerc turned from the crescent planet and its glowing hotspot to the entrance of the horseshoe. "Ms. Guo, what a pleasant surprise."

"Surprise?" She looked as demure as before. Her dress looked as pressed as it had when she'd walked in that morning. She stood with her arms folded and her gaze on the screen.

"I had assumed your routine, pre-scheduled trip would have ended, and you'd be flying back to St. Petersburg."

"I was leaving for my hotel when the alert about this—" She looked at the hotspot. "—came through from Randolph and Tung." Behind her, Hagerty's eyes had deeper bags under them than usual, and strands of his combover were out of place, like tracks merging in a railroad switchyard.

Meanwhile, Aggarwal waited in Leclerc's office, undoubtedly drinking more whisky. His respect for Guo bumped up a notch. So too did his dread of the thin ice under his career. Picking his words, he said, "I don't know anything more than you."

"You think this anomaly is a volcano?" she asked.

"Don't you?"

"The temperature is far too high," she said. "The hottest known terrestrial volcano never reached 2000 K, let alone 8000."

"I did not know you were a vulcanologist."

"I'm not."

Leclerc hooked his thumb over his shoulder, toward the screen. "Regardless, the hotspot isn't terrestrial."

"Perhaps," said Guo. "There is nothing else that might cause such a thing?"

"You speak as if you know the answer."

A smile teased her lips. Her gaze returned to the main screen. "I don't know anything more than you." Then voices burbled around the vast room and her smile drained away.

Leclerc twisted around. The hotspot extended a tiny blob. False color showed it was even brighter and hotter than the main body. The blob flickered on and off the screen. A glitch in the data? The interferometry array sometimes coughed up artefacts like that.

As he watched, the blob broke free. It moved away from the hotspot, flickering for a few moments, until it stayed lit. A single, actinic point. The hotspot extended another blob after it, more diffuse and much dimmer and cooler than the main body.

But the second blob could not catch up. The single point of light moved away from the hotspot.

Gaining speed every moment?

Leclerc's five-o'clock shadow stood up on his jaw and cheeks. A clammy feeling ran down the front of his neck. "Tung, show us the velocity of that moving point."

"Yes, sir." Tung hunched forward and worked the controls. A text box popped up and crawled across the main screen, keeping pace with the pinpoint of light. $1837\ m/s$ showed first. A moment later, the numbers jumped around. "It is difficult to measure."

"Do your best," Leclerc said. He rolled his lips in and out while his gaze stayed on the screen. Though the numbers fluctuated, the trend soon broke 1900. 2000.

"Tung, the acceleration as well."

Tung turned, face tight. "It is very difficult, sir. The velocity readings are too poor in quality to accurately calculate the derivative. Please do not expect correct numbers."

Hand at his side, Leclerc's fingers clawed the air. "I won't," he said, more sharply than he meant. He'd rather get imperfect data than no data at all. Then he turned to Randolph. "What was that?"

Randolph had watched the screen and muttered for a few seconds. "...seven mississippi, eight mississippi." He turned to Leclerc and Hagerty. "Velocity went up about 250 meters per second in about eight seconds. Give or take. That's an acceleration of about three gees."

The text box showed $2214\ m/s$ for an instant before the number fell back into a blur of digits. Tung hit some key with an emphatic clack and the text box grew, adding a line below. $31\ m/s^2$. "Proper calculations are in line with Randolph's guess."

Guo stepped forward with a swish of her dress. The reflected glow from the main screen filled her dark eyes. "The extremely bright object is accelerating?"

"Yes," said Hagerty and Leclerc at the same time.

"Thank you," Guo said over her shoulder to Hagerty, "but I asked Leclerc."

Hagerty made a strangled noise. He shuffled backward to the horseshoe's opening, and tugged on his upper lip as if it were made of pallid rubber.

Guo swung her gaze to Leclerc. "Volcanic ejecta could not do that, could they?"

Leclerc's mouth felt dry. "No."

Deadpan, she said, "Then it must be *Concordia*, mustn't it?"

It couldn't be. If their calculations were accurate, the ship would be on the other side of the planet. Even if they were badly wrong, and even if *Concordia* happened to pass through the line of sight between the hotspot and Earth, nothing about the pinpoint matched. The ship would orbit with a higher velocity and no acceleration.

If it couldn't be *Concordia*.... "Perhaps one of the landing craft," Leclerc managed. He wished he could hide for a moment and dab sweat off his scalp.

"I have no record that any landing craft was deployed to the middle of the supercontinent," Guo said. "And even at full thrust of their chemical rockets, the light and heat of a landing craft launch would not generate enough signal for our arrays to pick up."

Leclerc cast his gaze around the room. Concerned looks aimed everywhere, as if they ricocheted off the double-height walls. At the pinpoint on the main screen, speed now 3 klicks per second and rising. At Leclerc and the others inside the horseshoe. At a new arrival, coming in on the ground floor.

He pivoted. Just inside the main doors strode Aggarwal. His brown eyes showed no regard for the anomalous energies glimpsed across a chasm of light-years. Instead, he scowled at Leclerc.

"Let us talk privately," Guo said, voice solemn. She gestured toward the glass-walled sitting area under the stairs, at the back of the chamber.

"About?"

"About the thing we both know but have not admitted to one another." She didn't wait for a response, instead, set off. Hagerty took a step after her, but she halted him with a curt wave, without breaking stride. Next to her chin, the ends of her pageboy cut bobbed with each step.

Leclerc followed. Nothing seemed real. Energies neither nature nor man could unleash. Guo opening to him.

Aggarwal stopped athwart Guo's path. She stopped short. Leclerc halted next to her. His superior's bushy eyebrows bunched over his eyes like man-eating caterpillars preparing to strike.

"Goddam, what's this?"

"Mr. Leclerc and I are preparing to discuss this unexpected situation from Bravo Charlie. Would you care to join us?"

Aggarwal's scowl hardened. "I would, but Leclerc might feel he can't say too much."

"If you so choose," Guo said. She took a step along a path around him. Walking more quickly than he'd ever seen before. Leclerc avoided Aggarwal's gaze and moved after her.

"Hey, I was kidding. I wouldn't miss it for the world." Aggarwal hurried to catch up.

At the sitting area, Leclerc stepped past Guo and held the door open for her. Aggarwal pushed his way through after her. Leclerc opaqued the walls, pulled the door shut, locked it. Checked for security, then nodded to the others.

They already sat. Aggarwal slouched in one of the chairs, left ankle on right knee. The cuff of his pants leg gaped, showing a glimpse of a dark sock with worn elastic. He gave Leclerc a gimlet eye.

On the other side of the art installation, Guo sat alone on a sofa, back straight, knees together. Her weight barely dented the cushion. She glanced down and at an angle, studying some shell fragment or lost bit of a dead man's kit inside the glass box.

Leclerc took the chair to Aggarwal's left. Guo broke off from looking at the art installation and faced the two men.

"I am prepared to admit that the Traditionalist Coalition has received coded messages from Varanathan on *Concordia*," she said. "The messages pertain to the discovery of an alien presence on Bravo Charlie."

Aggarwal said nothing. Leclerc responded. "In exchange for what?"

"A full sharing of all private data each of our sides has received about the alien presence."

Leclerc's heart thumped. For the first time all day, he felt like he could inhale a full breath. He turned his head to Aggarwal and said, "I think we..."

"Like, what alien presence?"

Both Leclerc and Guo gave Aggarwal incredulous looks. "Do you wish to play such a game?" she asked.

"Game? I still have no clue what you're talking about."

Guo fixed her gaze on him for a moment. Then her narrow chin inscribed a short arc as she turned to Leclerc. "Perhaps the adults in the room should talk. We are agreed that the extremely bright object —" She broke off and studied the main screen, visible through the one-way opacity. "Your personnel have calculated the object's distance and altitude, now?"

Leclerc twisted in his seat. Leather squeaked under him. "They know what they're doing."

The pinpoint and the hotspot were tiny spots on the scale of the crescent world. The pinpoint crawled away so slowly Leclerc could not see its motion. Yet the text box now gave the elevation as 29 kilometers, the distance, 38 kilometers. Both numbers, plus velocity, climbing. Only the acceleration remained steady at about three gees.

"The accelerating object is not a natural phenomenon. It is not a landing craft. It is not *Concordia*. Accordingly, it has an alien origin."

Weight lifted from Leclerc's shoulders. Finally, they broke through the walls of Humanist vs. Traditionalist and reached some common ground.

A *thwack* came from his right. Aggarwal's fingernail popped lint off the leg of his slacks.

Leclerc's shoulders stiffened. He willed them to relax. What could Aggarwal do? Demote him, exile him, bring charges against him? Never another international vacation.

His breath caught. Never see Sybil again? He loved his wife....

...and her joke about Mondays held a grain of truth. Uranie, muse of astronomy, was his mistress. He would put his marriage at risk to spend an intimate moment with her. Guilt and shame trickled through him, but he knew himself well enough to accept the truth.

"I cannot speak for the Humanist Alliance, you understand."

"You are a scientist expressing a reasoned opinion."

Leclerc bowed his head and shut his eyes a moment. He opened them to find Guo regarding him. Her green and off-white yin-yang pendant stood out against the yellow floral print of her dress.

"It is an alien object," he said.

"Like, hypothetically." Aggarwal's brown eyes flicked between them. The cast of his thick eyebrows made Leclerc think of a billiards player reading angles.

Guo said, "Mr. Leclerc, I am also prepared to disclose the following, as relayed to us by Varanathan—"

"Relayed to you? How?" Aggarwal gave her an arrogant look. "If you don't tell us how, we'll assume you're spreading disinformation."

"Before the ship departed, we worked out code phrases related to classic novels he would supposedly read during the mission. The ones in question relate to a series called the Raj Quartet. Written by an Englishman about that country's colonial rule over India."

Leclerc shook his head, his grin rueful. "I suspected as much."

Aggarwal quirked his mouth like he'd taken a sour bite. "Which phrases? Like, word for word. We have to, you know, corroborate what you tell us."

"The code book is stored only in hard copy in St. Petersburg. I do not have it memorized. I can paraphrase the meanings we extracted from his messages."

"Please do," Leclerc said.

"The ship detected alien objects in the desert in the middle of the supercontinent. I do not know the precise location relative to the hotspot." She looked up and through the glass wall, as if to make sure the hotspot had not vanished.

Leclerc followed her gaze. His landed on the text box accompanying the pinpoint. Velocity, elevation, altitude all increasing. The pinpoint would soon reach orbit.

A clammy feeling shivered up his legs.

Would it stop there?

He turned his head back as Guo added, "A team of six personnel, three from each faction, journeyed to the surface. They found a buried alien structure. No aliens alive, but they gathered enough evidence to conclude the aliens were not native to New Eden, pardon me, Bravo Charlie."

Aggarwal peered at her as if he doubted every word. "How can they tell dead aliens didn't come from Four Freedoms?"

Leclerc rubbed his hands together, trying to keep warm. The glass walls rendered the sitting area too cold in winter and too hot in summer. At least the poor climate control encouraged them to get to the point.

He and Guo, at least. Aggarwal knew, from Sandford's abstract art backdrops, the aliens originated off the planet. He and Leclerc had discussed as much half a dozen times. So why did he dither over unimportant points?

Because he wanted to gauge how much she knew, and compare it to Varanathan's transmissions. Determine the other side's capabilities, and perhaps accuse her later of holding something back. It made sense, in the inexorable logic of superpower relations.

Leclerc stole another glance at the pinpoint. How important were superpower relations, now?

"We did not establish a code phrase for him to tell us that," Guo said. "We trusted his people to figure out how through their own devices. We are certain Varanathan's conclusion is correct. Which brings up the next question."

Leclerc voiced it. "If not Bravo Charlie, from where did the aliens come?"

"Think through the answer," Guo said.

He shut his eyes. The triple-star Alpha Centauri system showed itself in his imagination. "No other planet in orbit around A, B, or Prox could have been habitable within the last hundred million years or more. If ever."

"Hence," said Guo, "the aliens undertook an interstellar journey. Which means they had propulsion systems as good as *Concordia*'s." She pointed with her narrow chin at the pinpoint on the main screen. "Or better."

Aggarwal snorted out a breath. "So that's why your man

Varanathan, like, shut down comms. He wanted to launch a coo-duh-mane. Knock out Sandford and our people. Take the alien tech for himself. And you."

Guo kept her placid gaze on Leclerc. "I surmise Sandford had orders to do the same, if the situation warranted it."

Aggarwal shot out his hand. "Don't answer that."

Leclerc's eye wrinkled in a wry smile. "I would make the same surmise if I were on your side of the table."

"We understand each other," Guo said.

"You came here today because you believed Varanathan had seized control of the ship and the alien technology," Leclerc said.

Guo dipped her head in a slow nod. "Our watch officer last Friday evening fed word up through our channels that the loss of contact appeared suspiciously favorable for the Traditionalist side. I came here with expectations of victory."

Leclerc turned his head. Hagerty leaned against the side of the horseshoe, staring glumly at the opaqued walls of the sitting area. Everyone else watched the main screen.

From the pinpoint's velocity, it had nearly reached orbit.

"Now," said Leclerc, "you are not so certain."

Guo's hand reached for her jade and porcelain pendant. Slender fingers twisted it, winding and unwinding her necklace chain. "That vessel is of alien origin. Who or what is piloting it?"

A chuckle came from Aggarwal. "Looks like you, you know, bit off more than you can chew. And now you need our help."

"I am not a fool," Guo said. "We believed the aliens to be dead. I have no reason to doubt Varanathan and the ground expedition on that point. Did a colony survive by hiding even farther out of sight? Or through suspended animation? Or is that vessel an autonomous machine?"

A possibility came to Leclerc. Did Guo's spirit of cooperation covered an effort to tease intel from them? "Perhaps the ground expedition is flying it."

She held a flat stare on him... then gave a brief smile. "A little humor." The smile faded. Her fingers kept twisting her pendant. Her forearm pressed against her chest, as if to shield herself from the worst explanations for the pinpoint of light and heat. "But impossible. Isn't it?"

"Of course," Leclerc said.

"Sandford communicated no details about what the ground expedition found, or learned?"

She hadn't. Despite Aggarwal sitting next to him, still scowling under bushy black eyebrows, Leclerc wanted to speak only the truth. "No."

Guo angled her head. Her dark eyes regarded him as he met and held her gaze. "You are being honest with me."

Leclerc shrugged. "What, then, is our hypothesis? The ground expedition roused a dormant alien ship?"

"The evidence so far points to that. Not under Varanathan's control. Or anyone's." Her head snapped up to the main screen.

Leclerc turned. It took only a moment to see what had caught her attention. The pinpoint had vanished from the visible spectrum over the planet. Only flickers in the infrared marked its position, in the moments when the array could distinguish its internal temperature from Bravo Charlie's warm night.

Flickers and the text box. Altitude two hundred kilometers, speed six thousand meters per second.

Leclerc knew instantly what the numbers meant. "The alien ship entered Bravo Charlie orbit."

"Where will it go from there?" Guo said. She clutched her pendant tighter. "Will it come to Earth?"

Aggarwal's eyebrows rose. He studied the planet on the main screen. The hotspot continued to glow in the middle of the red desert. "Don't bother asking Leclerc."

"Why not?"

"Because he's about to resign his post, you know? Unless he wants to, like, take over the ground station at Diego Garcia."

She arched her eyebrow. To Leclerc, she said, "He wants to punish you for admitting Sandford sent coded messages to you?"

Leclerc rolled his wrists in a shrug. "In sum, yes."

Guo gave Aggarwal a cold look. "We do not accept."

"Like, you don't have any say in our personnel decisions."

While her gaze remained fixed on Aggarwal, she extended one finger toward the main screen. "An alien ship launched from the surface of Bravo Charlie. It could have set off for Earth over four years ago. At this moment, it could be mere months from us. Coming with unknown intentions and capabilities that could devastate your half of the world as easily as ours. Leclerc understands the situation. Do you?"

Aggarwal crossed his arms and hunched, scowling, over them.

"Do you need to save face inside your hierarchy regarding the formal protest the Coalition announced it would file?" Guo asked. She released her pendant. Her hands rested in her lap. "I will, how does one say, put egg on my face? I will enter onto the record that I falsified the allegations against Leclerc and you. Sandford never communicated to you through coded messages. And then we will proceed to deal with this situation like adults."

Aggarwal leaned back. His arms flopped to the chair next to his thighs. His scowl drifted to the main screen, and the text box crawling at thousands of kilometers per hour. And then the scowl faded, breaking into an expression hinting at the cunning behind the California slang and the Humanist rhetoric.

"You know, if there's an alien ship with unknown intentions coming our way I don't want to rock the boat. Leclerc, we don't want you to resign, got it? Your place is here."

Leclerc resisted the urge to dab cold sweat from his scalp. "I will do my duties to the mission and to the Humanist Alliance."

"Bueno." Aggarwal stood and stretched his arms toward the sitting area's glass ceiling. One elbow crackled with the motion while his brown eyes studied the main screen. "Looks like, right now, we've got nothing to do but wait."

Leclerc stood. Time to escape this hothouse of senior bureaucrats knife-fighting with words and sharp looks. Time to finish his paperwork and get home, to a warm meal and the bed he shared with Sybil. "Mr. Aggarwal, Dr. Guo, if you'll excuse me."

Guo stood too. "Of course. For now." Light from above glossed on the jade side of her pendant. She glanced at the main screen, sending a ripple through her black hair. "We might have to work together much more in the future."

CHAPTER 6

16 OCTOBER 2127 (EARTH REFERENCE FRAME) | 17 DECEMBER 2125
(*NAPOLEON* REFERENCE FRAME)

FIVE HUMAN BEINGS floated weightless in the alien chapel.

They couldn't be certain the largest room on the ship served that purpose. Though the Octaliens left behind voluminous writings, on the walls of both this ship and the facility they'd buried in the desert of the planet below, they spoke only of science and history. Not faith. Whatever god they worshipped, and how they did so, died with the last of their species, in the underground facility over a million years ago.

But to Harrison Jaeger and the others, *chapel* seemed the best guess. The ceiling of the cubical room, roughly fifteen feet from the floor, would have towered high above the diminutive Octaliens. A metallic tree ran along one wall and extended branches into the room. Twenty-three branches, a prime number. Another prime, nineteen, the number of bioluminescent lighting discs arranged in a bullseye pattern. Under gravity or thrust, the lighting discs would be on the ceiling, and the tree would rise toward them.

Along the walls, though faded by deep time, life-sized murals showed the ship's alien builders against a background of dark green splotches under a blue-black sky. Though their hairless, featherless skin blended into the color palette of green behind them, each one stood out. Sixty-one of them, each about two feet tall, with four arms ending in two fingers each. A few more males than females. Jaeger could tell them apart because the males were an inch or two taller and a couple of shades lighter.

Their eight fingers, and corresponding use of a base-eight numbering system, led the humans to call them *Octaliens*. Annike Ingvarsson's best translation of their name for themselves was *we-who-are*.

Were, now. The name hadn't kept dueling factions on their homeworld from blowing it up while this ship undertook its first journey, from their unidentified G8 main-sequence star to Alpha Centauri.

The bitterest rivals were those in the same niche. Marie d'Arbaud, the biochemist, had said that, months ago on the surface, and it stuck in Jaeger's mind ever since.

Hell, it might have even inspired the plan.

Whatever rivalry had driven the Octaliens to use weapons of mass destruction on themselves was absent in the mural. Most of the Octaliens stood on two legs and held one another's hands. Along the balcony, near the upper doors, where dark green reached for the ceiling, mothers sat on branches, sinuous tails wrapped around for support, infants cradled by three of their four arms. Every Octalien's two front eyes looked up at the metallic tree. Impossible to read from their expressions whatever emotions they'd felt, but their poses seemed reverent.

Above them, on the wall opposite the tree, a group of thirteen bioluminescent discs, coin-sized, formed a constellation of bright stars in a twilight sky. With a little imagination, you could see the thirteen discs forming an Octalien with arms raised and fingers open to wisdom from on high.

Jaeger recalled messages laser-etched in rust-free alloys in the buried alien base. That wisdom had helped inspire the plan too.

After seven weeks in orbit, the ship was no longer fully alien. Jaeger and the others added human touches here and there, between long working hours, extruded meals of tasteless pap, and not enough rack time. Throughout the ship, chapel included.

Marie and Andrew McIlroy, geologist and now her boyfriend, deciphered the instructions for the Octalien nanotech well enough to produce LED panels. Jaeger and Annike mounted them on the ceiling, making up for discs that lost their bioluminescence thousands of years before. Ulanovas, the Lithuanian pilot, ran power cables along the bulkheads to a makeshift breaker box and wired them in while Jaeger and Annike glued them in place behind him. Bulkheads throughout the ship looked like they had varicose veins.

In the chapel, more LEDs glowed with cool twinkles on the tree's alloy branches. White reflections glimmered on plastic ornaments of red and green. A week before Christmas, ship's time.

A day before departure.

They floated between the metallic tree and the images of Octaliens. They aligned themselves with the direction that would be *up* when under thrust. A fist-sized recycling bag drifted in the air. Visible through translucent plastic, crumbs of French bread from their sandwiches and smears of chocolate mousse from dessert clung to the inside. "Thanks for getting some real food out of the fab," Jaeger said.

Marie shook her head. A wisp of hair escaped her graying brown bun. "There is so much we cannot synthesize yet," she said in her accent from southern France. "And no kitchen to cook it in."

Next to Marie, McIlroy shifted, bumped into her. His lively eyes regarded her. "Yet." He turned to the rest of them. "We know how to code any human design into the Octalien nanofab." He scratched his trimmed brown beard. "The only thing holding us back is knowing the human designs."

Jaeger nodded his head. They'd been chased into the ship with the clothes on their backs and the data in their wearables. Fab designs were locked up in the mainframes at the ground expedition stations on the surface and on crippled, muted *Concordia*. "We have time to come up with designs of our own."

Plenty of it. Three-plus years of relativistic travel time back to Earth.

Ulanovas tossed his head to sweep sandy blond hair away from his eyes. "I know you will make better things. Even cold food is better than what the ship first gave us, okay?"

"And speaking for getting real things from the fab...." Jaeger gestured to McIlroy.

The geologist reached for a backpack drifting in the air near his knee. He unzipped the pack and pulled out transparent squeezebulbs filled with red liquid. "Marie's latest invention."

Marie's eyes, usually soft, hardened in mock outrage. "This wine is plonk," she said. "I said it was not good enough to drink."

A grin showed itself through McIlroy's brown beard. "Might could be it's not up to snuff for a refined Provençal palate, Dr. d'Arbaud...." His quiet voice pronounced her surname correctly, *dar-bow*, but drawled it out. He extended a hand toward Jaeger and hammed up his accent even more. "But you have here two Texans with no fancy tastes."

She answered him with a raised eyebrow and a quirk of her mouth. Then she and McIlroy both laughed.

Jaeger put on an apologetic look. "I told Mac we needed something to toast with." He raised his squeezebulb. "To all we've done."

Annike raised one slender arm. "*Skaal.*" She glanced at Jaeger, warmth in her fair face and uncommon brown eyes. Her skin was alabaster, save for the mole on her cheek. Her blond ponytail bobbed in the air with every slight motion of her head.

All five raised their bulbs. Jaeger squirted the wine into his mouth. Too sweet at first, then its tannins punched him in the mouth. He stifled a pucker.

Marie turned her soft eyes on him. "I told you it was plonk."

He coughed and thumped the flat of his hand on his chest. "I'm amazed you got anything drinkable out of the fab. I know you'll refine it, but keep the formula. We need to drink it again, on special occasions."

"Atrocious Wine Day is to become a holiday?"

"No. But maybe Launch-mas Eve should be. We'll want something to remind us how far we've come."

"Hear, hear," said McIlroy. He snuggled against Marie.

A warmth in Jaeger's chest dispelled the wine's sour taste and the perpetual floppy stomach of free fall. He gave each of the others a warm look. Humanist, Traditionalist, the old labels no longer existed. The five of them had come together for a common purpose. To do on a greater scale, intentionally, and with selfless motives, what the ship's namesake, Napoleon, had accidentally provoked through his arrogance and ambition.

To unite humankind against them.

Ulanovas reached for an alloy branch near his head. Steady in air, he cleared his throat and brandished his bulb. "One more toast, then I must stop drinking, okay?"

"Toast away," said McIlroy.

The Lithuanian regarded them. "To all we have left to do."

A moment of silence, then Jaeger added "Indeed" to the chorus of toasts in multiple languages.

Solemn toasts. Ulanovas was right about how much they had to do. Building precision weapons, deploying them on *Napoleon*'s hull, selecting targets, inflicting minimal damage on Earth's innocent billions while creating maximum fear in the Trad and Humanist leadership....

Jaeger squirted wine into his mouth. It tasted as bad the second time around.

Annike drifted closer to him. Their bodies bumped, thighs and upper arms.

He smiled at her. The simple touch put Ulanovas's toast in perspective.

The wine would get better. The food too. They would humanize the ship. They would build the most precise weapons and prep the best mission plan they could. They had thirty-eight months.

Plenty of time before they came in war for all mankind.

Ulanovas reached for the recycling bag. He peeled back the sticky flap holding it closed and dropped his squeezebulb in. "Jaeger," the pilot said, and Jaeger mused for a moment how good it felt when everyone pronounced his name *Yay-grr*, "Don't drink too much, okay? I still need you to start the engines in the morning."

Jaeger swallowed one sour squirt. Grimacing, he said, "Drinking too much won't be a problem."

Ulanovas nodded. "Good night, all." He pushed off the metallic branch on a vector to one of the doorways on the lower level. He grabbed the frame with both hands and pulled himself through. His long wide boots disappeared from view.

Silence held in the chapel, save for the rustle of plastic as Marie gathered up their squeezebulbs for recycling. A drawn look on her face brought Jaeger drifting closer. Marie said to Annike, "What's your assessment?" Marie nodded her head toward the doorway where Ulanovas had left.

Annike blinked. Jaeger too. He rarely thought about her original, primary role on the *Concordia* mission, Humanist psych officer.

"Good enough."

Jaeger shifted, touching different parts of Annike's arm and leg with his. "He's the only one who didn't find somebody."

Marie nodded briefly, but kept her attention on Annike. "How long since he joked about aliens visiting Earth in ancient times?"

"Not long enough," McIlroy said with a grin. It soon got lost in his brown beard.

Jaeger's thoughts traveled similar paths. If their pilot's mental health deteriorated in seven years of round-trip flight—

—if anybody's did—

"We have to keep busy," he said. He turned his gaze to McIlroy. "On your side of the inner Texan border, did they say 'The devil finds work for idle hands'?"

"No. We're all good Humanists. We don't practice religion or golf." He mimed a backswing. Then the humorous twinkle in his eyes went away. "Work is a good prescription. I reckon Dr. Ingvarsson would agree?"

"Work is a positive influence on mental well-being," Annike said, "if one has a purpose behind it."

McIlroy scratched his beard in contemplation. "I reckon he does."

"The mission," Annike said. "'He who has a why to live for can bear almost any how.'"

Marie considered. "So do we all." She drifted closer to McIlroy. He turned to her with a smile.

Jaeger turned to Annike. He raised the back of his hand to her cheek and trailed his fingers over the mole there. They all had work, for a higher purpose. The four people in the room each had a lover to live for, too.

On the walls, the faded Octaliens looked through the humans, to the tree behind them, under the gaze of a prophet or a god in their image glittering in the first nighttime stars.

CHAPTER 7

7 MARCH 2132

Low CLOUDS BLOTTED the sun and cast a gray gloom on the English countryside. The sport utility vehicle slowed for the final turn onto the lane.

Leclerc glanced over fields of dull brown to their destination eight hundred meters away.

Cheltenford Hall sprawled along a low rise. The country house lay like a mythical beast cobbled together from the body parts of multiple animals. One wing showed exposed, slanted timbers infilled with white brick. Another, where dormer windows peered through a steep-sloped roof, reminded him of France.

The vehicle turned under a wrought iron gate. The lane's pavement whispered under the tires. From his rear-facing front seat, he could no longer see the country house. Elms lined the lane, extending gnarled, leafless branches over the roadway.

Gloomy day.

Gloomy company, as well. Next to Leclerc sat Evans, blond and tanned as usual, but head down. Pretending to be engrossed in a private virtual, rather than reproach himself on Leclerc's gaze. His attempted coup two months prior still left a sour taste in Leclerc's mouth.

Across from them, Aggarwal knitted his bushy eyebrows at the country house.

The fear people showed Aggarwal at mission control, Aggarwal showed the men and women waiting for them.

In front of the house, the SUV turned onto a circular driveway. It braked silently at the front entrance. In this part of the structure, tightly fitted gray stone showed the hall's origins as a medieval fortress. Above the double doors, upright slashes filled with mortar and brick marked centuries-old arrow slits.

The SUV popped its doors. Cool, humid air crept into the cabin. Leclerc beckoned for Aggarwal to climb out first. As much to delay his exposure to the weather as to defer to his superior.

Leclerc could only delay a few seconds. Standing on the pavement, he pulled his overcoat tighter and shuddered. Clammy air wormed inside his collar. The clouds looked ready to spit on them at any moment. The honest, dry cold of his home this morning seemed almost as distant as the tropical beach waiting for him that summer.

If he could still take a vacation, after today's meeting.

After the latest news from Bravo Charlie.

Evans climbed out last. He folded his arms and stamped his foot. The SUV, oblivious to the cold and gloom, tucked in its doors and slipped farther down the lane, along the front of the brick and timber wing. Bound for wherever it would park. Its silvery paint and swooping lines made it look like an interloper against the ancient backdrop of the country house.

No escaping the meeting, now.

Aggarwal regarded Leclerc. "I do the talking unless someone asks you a direct science question. If they do, stay out of the weeds. No one's got time for details, you know?"

"I understand. And Evans?"

"He's part of my posse, you know?"

"I can't say I do."

Aggarwal grimaced. "He isn't here to talk. He's here to make it look like I've got the entire team on this."

Evans opened his mouth, plainly to protest being talked about as if he weren't there. But Aggarwal strode toward the front entrance and Leclerc raised an eyebrow at him.

He responded with a tight-lipped nod. He bowed his head and followed Aggarwal and Leclerc.

The doors swung inward. Two of the country house's staff waited on the marble floor, under a high ceiling crossed by exposed beams. The staffers, one man, one woman, looked like fraternal twins. Deep blue suits, unlined faces, arms straight at their sides.

"Welcome to Cheltenford Hall," the man said. He spoke like a news reader, as if he used a cleaver to separate one word from the next. "Utter the words 'assistance please' in public space and a staff member will attend to you within thirty seconds." His green eyes lingered a moment over Evans's. From that, and the way the woman canted her hip a few inches toward Aggarwal, they hinted just how many needs they would attend to.

The woman straightened her posture. Her voice was cool and smooth as whipped cream. "Your party has reserved Conference Room A. The others are finishing their luncheon and will meet you there within fifteen minutes."

"Follow us, please," said the man.

Heels clacked on marble. The man and woman led the way through a maze of rooms on the ground floor. At times, one of the staffers turned a filigreed knob to open a door, then stood aside to close it after they passed.

The rooms repeated a template. Walls in pastel shades. On plinths between the windows, vases with spidery cracks held roses flown in from subtropical climes that morning. Sitting areas of high-backed wooden furniture in some antique style faced tongues of flame flickering in white brick fireplaces. Just one settee or divan probably cost more than Leclerc's car. And did the fireplaces faintly hiss? Yes, the unmistakable sound of natural gas, trickling carbon dioxide into the atmosphere.

Of course, those who owned and used Cheltenford Hall were exempted from the greenhouse gas regulations imposed on the rest of the Humanist world.

What is permitted to Jove is denied to oxen....

Their guides led them to the mock Tudor wing, then up stairs with treads like saddles, the middle of each marble piece worn down by countless feet over centuries. Although the sounds of other people, staffers and guests, drifted down the halls or through the open transom windows above the doors, they saw no one else.

Rumor had it the place served a clientele of the merely rich, to throw Trad spies off the scent of what took place here.

Finally, the man slipped a ring of keys from his pocket and unlocked a door lined with infilled gold before opening it for them.

A spacious room greeted Leclerc and his traveling companions. A fireplace of uneven stones in one corner gave more light than heat. The wing's slanted timbers showed through to the interior walls. Paintings of old English country life hung between triangular picture windows. The tall panes gave views onto a garden of flagstone paths and planter boxes raised fifty centimeters above the ground. Half a mile distant, their silvery SUV drove through the wide doors of a barn in the same half-timbered Tudor style as their wing of the house.

Closer, in the garden, a woman in a pantsuit, like an African sister to Leclerc's female guide, scowled at a team of spidery robots tilling the soil of the boxes. The motion of rotating blades bristled at the robot's mouths.

Their guides took their leave. They shut the door but did not lock it.

The room could be comfortable. But the modular tables set on hidden casters had arranged themselves into a single long one at the head of the room. Six swivel chairs with thick cushions waited behind the long table. Clusters of personal items showed each of the swivel chairs belonged to someone. Styluses, medicine bottles, cups of water, an ink pen and a block of paper.

Leclerc looked over the herringbone pattern of the polished parquet floor, like a basketball court or a ballroom.

There were no other chairs.

"They're making us stand?" Evans asked.

"We're not here to chit-chat, you know?" Aggarwal paced to the windows and stared at the gardens. Behind his back, his hands flexed into and out of fists. "We answer their questions and if we have to, cover our asses. Then they tell us what to do and we go do it."

Evans angled his head. "Why do we need a CYA routine?"

Aggarwal didn't reply. Evans turned his lanky frame to Leclerc. Puzzlement was a rare visitor to his tanned face.

Leclerc spoke with a tinge of pity. Before you tried to unseat me, you should have thought about the sharks you would swim with. "It is human nature, when one receives bad news, to shoot the messenger."

"But they know we aren't responsible for...."

Footsteps sounded in the hallway. Aggarwal pivoted.

Those who sat behind the table came in. As they filed into place, the door swung itself shut behind them.

Leclerc studied them. In the middle of the group, one familiar face, Neville, the Pan-European representative on the Humanist high council. Large brown eyes too close together over a long and narrow nose. Tanned face and hands visible above the unbuttoned popped collar of his silk shirt and the rolled back cuffs of his tweed jacket. The creases across his high forehead and the wisps of gray in his hair at his temples made him look mature yet still vigorous. The people's representative, accustomed to the spotlight.

The other five, three men and two women, ranged from youthful to wrinkled. Clothes trendy to nerdy. One lean-faced man in jeans and a black T-shirt blazoned with the logo of an ancient rock band. Apparently he held such a high position he could come to work larping as someone from the climatepunk era. One woman with a blond beehive of hair, misty blue eyes, sea-green blouse, a gaudy orange cravat. A man in suit and tie whose shades of gray and black seemed to blend into the background. All strangers to Leclerc's sight. He knew in an instant they would not introduce themselves.

Likely, from their positions in the shadows, all were far more powerful than the mere representative in the center.

Aggarwal padded back to Leclerc and Evans. His mouth was tight but his bushy eyebrows were up, as if he were a child about to swear his innocence about the broken jar of cookie crumbs.

"Remember," he muttered. Only speak when asked. And only about the science, at a high level.

In Leclerc's peripheral vision, the senior bureaucrats took their seats. Like judges on a panel in the barbarous past, voting to send a scapegoat to the guillotine.

He nodded back to Aggarwal. The less he had to speak with the gray eminences on the other side of the table, the better.

From his seat in the center, Neville shook a blue medicine tablet from the bottle to his palm. He popped it into his mouth and chased it with water, then set bottle and cup aside. He peered down his nose. He spoke English in some drawling, upper crust accent. Perhaps his ancestors had owned Cheltenford Hall, before the Humanist power structure bought them out. "Aggarwal. Gentlemen. You know why we've called you here."

"The alien launch," Aggarwal said.

The man in the T-shirt swung his gaze back from the window as if annoyed he had to speak. Some American accent, dripping with sarcasm. "Oh, *that's* why."

Aggarwal dropped his gaze to the floor and shuffled back half a step. He mumbled, "Sorry, Mr. Memford."

Neville went on smoothly. "We've seen the video Leclerc sent us. Firstly, walk us through it, to make sure we understand what we see."

At the end of the table nearest the door, the man in the gray suit and tie lifted one hand off the tabletop just far enough to twitch his fingers.

A virtual window popped into Leclerc's vision, projected onto the back wall above Neville. The virtual window showed in miniature what he'd seen on the main screen at mission control.

A still frame. Centered on Bravo Charl—no, facing these people, only think of it as Four Freedoms. The planet showed mostly daytime on its watery hemisphere. A sliver of green to the left, a crescent of night on the right. Clouds dotted the sunlit ocean, chief among them a tropical storm gyring near the equator.

He glanced at the timestamp out of habit. No need.

He knew what he was about to see again.

"What are we looking at?" Neville asked. "Tell me as if I were a child, if you would."

Aggarwal cleared his throat and took a half step forward. "This is a composite of vi—"

"Were you there?" The blonde with the orange cravat had a lilting voice and an accent from somewhere in Eastern Europe. She sat between Neville and the man in gray. "At mission control when Leclerc and Evans received this data?"

Aggarwal blinked a few times. "No, but I—"

"Thank you," she said brightly. She leaned to peer around Aggarwal. "Mr. Leclerc, tell us."

Leclerc shuffled forward and to the side, more fully into her view. He cleared his throat and hoped sweat wouldn't shine on his bald scalp. "It was last Thursday, 28th Feb—"

At the other end of the table, next to the window, the sarcastic American, Memford, knuckled his chest through the lightning bolt down the middle of his T-shirt. "Too bad there's no timestamp to tell us that."

The blonde shifted to face him. "He's doing what Neville asked for," she said. Her tone and body language showed Neville was to be humored, as if he were a senile uncle who would leave them millions in his will.

"I'll thank you to remember that," Neville chimed in, but Memford had already leaned back in his chair.

Leclerc's gaze darted between them, until the blonde gave a little nod with a sweet smile on her face.

Sweet as the apple in Eden.

"A week ago, 28th February, 1024 hours," said Leclerc. "As Mr. Aggarwal alluded, this view combines visual and infrared observations of Four Freedoms from an array of platforms on the ground, near Earth, and in solar orbits up to three AU from the Sun."

His cheeks felt warm. Three astronomical units? Should he say half a billion kilometers instead?

He glanced at Neville. The man nodded, at least pretending to follow along.

"That's a sufficient level of detail," the blonde said.

Neville nodded. Memford in the rock band T-shirt snorted out a breath.

Leclerc raised his finger to the virtual window. "If I may?" he asked. His gaze turned from Neville to the blonde. Where was the gray man? Next to her.

The man in gray bobbed his chin, flexed his fingers.

An icon joined the status bar in Leclerc's view. He now had telestrator privileges.

He circled a dot to the right of the planet, two hundred kilometers above the surface. "This marks the alien ship in orbit. Please play the video, normal speed."

If the gray man moved his fingers, Leclerc couldn't tell. The video advanced. The dot wavered in brightness, and for a few frames, winked out of existence.

"Tell me," Neville said. "Do they have stealth capabilities?"

So foolish a question, Leclerc's mouth gaped. After a couple of blinks, he managed, "We don't expect so. We consider the variable appearance to more likely arise from limitations in our observation technology."

"Yes, of course," Neville said, a strain of disappointment in his voice.

Disappointment? From watching too much fanciful cinema about alien contact. There could be no other explanation. Neville couldn't want the aliens to cloak their ship in stealth. No one could be that foolish.

Aggarwal cleared his throat. "Goes without saying, we will, like, keep monitoring to see if perhaps they have stealth." He raised a thick eyebrow at Leclerc.

"Of course, yes," Leclerc said.

Inside the circle, the dot suddenly solidified into a bright ring. Aggarwal's little bureaucratic games now seemed irrelevant. "This is the moment the alien ship began firing its main engines."

"It didn't just turn on some lights?" Neville asked.

The blonde smiled. "Like a giant selfie light ring?"

"Precisely, Ms. Rubik," said Neville. "Perhaps they needed to illuminate something in orbit."

The blonde, Rubik, gave Leclerc a partial wink. "I'm sure Mr. Leclerc has his reasons for concluding they fired their engines."

"Look at the night side of the planet, please."

The power brokers on the other side of the table angled their heads at their own private virtual displays. Expressions ranged from puzzled to bored.

They didn't know what to look for. Leclerc telestrated more. His finger sketched an oval in the crescent of night time sea. In the center of the oval, bright gray streaked across the dark ocean. The streak slashed horizontally from the middle of the crescent past the limb of the world. Above and below, the edges of the streak faded into the full dark of the planet's night.

"The ship's engines are so powerful," Leclerc said, "their reflection on the planet is brighter than a full moon."

The hatchet-faced American, Memford, peered at him. "It's not *Concordia?*"

"No. We know *Concordia*'s exhaust is primarily helium at—" The precise temperatures were more detail than they wanted. "Is very hot helium. It would have characteristic emission spectra. We do not see it."

Memford crossed his arms in front of his chest, cutting off the bottom half of the faux-distressed letters on his T-shirt. "I don't *see* anything."

Leclerc's mouth worked for a moment. "Your pardon?"

"I'm from Missou-rah." A nonsense phrase in a cornpone accent. Memford's face hardened even more than usual. His voice returned to normal. "Show me."

Leclerc patted his scalp. Clammy but not sweaty. "Evans, pull up the spectral comparisons."

Evans hunched his shoulders, tapped and swiped the air. Leclerc turned his way, less to pressure him than to avoid the knife-like stare from the sarcastic American.

"It may take them a couple of minutes" Aggarwal said. "We take your security demands seriously. The data is all encrypted at mission control and, you know, they've got authentication hoops to jump through."

"Got it," mumbled Evans. He shared the comparison with Leclerc. The spectra tiled themselves to the left of the video of the alien ship.

Leclerc glanced over the pair of images. Exactly what they needed. "Good work." He raised his voice for Aggarwal and the power brokers to hear. "It's ready. May I push it to you?"

The blonde, Rubik, smiled. The man in gray lifted his index finger off the table.

Leclerc tapped a virtual *send* button floating in the air. The pair of images duplicated itself and flew to everyone else in the room. He gave the others a second to open the images before speaking.

"The upper spectrum is taken from observations of *Concordia*'s exhaust, averaged from the ship's Sol system departure to its turnover halfway to Alpha Centauri. We processed out the Doppler shift from relativistic effects. Characteristic helium emission features are here, here, and here." He circled peaks and valleys with his finger.

"The lower spectrum is from the exhaust of the object seen in the video. The two spectra are at the same scale and are vertically aligned." His finger circled the entire flat emission plateau. "As you can see, the object's exhaust emits at constant amplitude at all wavelengths."

Neville frowned. "It looks like a straight line."

Rubik rolled her misty blue eyes, then gave Leclerc an encouraging smile.

He put on a self-deprecating face. "I suppose it does. I hadn't seen that before." His smile dwindled. "I trust you can see that *Concordia*'s exhaust could not look like this. From that we conclude that it is indeed the alien ship."

"Thank you," said Rubik. She arched an eyebrow at Memford, then asked Leclerc, "What kind of engine could produce an exhaust looking like that?"

His chest tightened. "An engine that uses light for thrust."

She angled her head at him. "This troubles you?"

"Light is inefficient reaction mass. To generate the thrust needed to propel a ship as large as this one appears to be requires energy sources unavailable to us."

"Yet," Rubik affably said, as if a team in a lab was an equation away from discovering it.

Leclerc's face remained sober. "Or ever." His gaze roved the table. From their expressions, none of them grasped exactly what that meant. "This ship uses—" He waggled his hand. "—perhaps a thousand times as much power as *Concordia*."

Eyebrows went up. Faces closed in. *Concordia*'s power plant could level a city. The alien ship's could sterilize a continent.

The man in gray spoke, in a voice as bland as his attire. Even his Latin American accent sounded boring, but the weight in his words overcame everything else. "And it's coming here."

CHAPTER 8

7 MARCH 2132

FOR A MOMENT, the only sounds came from the hissing fireplace in the corner and low clips from the gardening robots outside. Eyebrows rose. Yellow and orange motion of hair and cravat as Rubik pivoted to face him. A jaundiced scowl from Memford in his rock band T-shirt.

Leclerc bowed. "So it appears."

Memford's face slashed the air. "Oh really."

Voice wobbling, Leclerc said, "Allow me to show you." He raised his finger to the video of the planet. The ring of light from the alien ship had crept toward the right edge of the screen. The reflection of the ship's exhaust on the night-dark sea had faded inside the telestrated oval, but it remained horizontal in the field of view.

"We look at Four Freedoms and the rest of the Alpha Centauri B system from above its ecliptic plane."

In response to a blank look from Neville, Leclerc made a fist with his left hand. "Picture this as the star." He circled the tip of his right index finger around it. He kept his finger in a nearly-vertical plane. "And this, the planet."

Leclerc continued, his voice more confident. "All of B's planets and significant asteroids lie in the same plane. If the ship were traveling somewhere in the Alpha Centauri B system, its exhaust would reflect in the same plane as well."

"And the ship would not show a symmetrical ring of exhaust," said the man in gray.

"Yes," Leclerc said. Across the table, knitted eyebrows and crossed arms made him scramble for a better way to explain. "Picture a hand torch. Evans, what's the American word?"

"Flashlight?"

"Thank you." He mimed holding one, then turned it sideways. "If the ship journeyed at an angle to our line of sight, we'd see more exhaust to one side or the other." With his other hand, he gestured as if light spewed out of the pretend flashlight.

He then turned it to shine on him. With his other thumb and forefinger, he made a circle slightly larger around the non-existent flashlight lamp. "But to see exhaust light as we do, it must be coming directly at us."

Neville lifted his chin to peer down his nose at the virtual video. "But the ship is moving out of our line of sight to Four Freedoms. That means it's moving at an angle away from Earth."

"The planet is moving in its orbit away from the direct line between us and the ship. Our observation array tracks the planet, not the ship."

"We should change that," Neville said, voice confident. Then he shrank back and glanced to the figures to both his sides.

"The masses would get wind of something if we stopped watching the planet," said Memford. "Too many schools show the video in their science classes."

Rubik looked at Aggarwal. "You thought of that?"

"There's a two-week delay before public affairs releases video from mission control. We'll edit out the engine burn, same as we edited out the volcanic anomaly back in January."

Neville's face looked pinched, as if the masses were gnats buzzing around his head. "Do we have enough cameras to both watch the planet and track the ship?"

"I believe so," said Rubik. To Leclerc, she said, "Correct?"

He nodded. "The resolution depends on the distance between our telescopes, much more than the number. We can repurpose some of them as a second array to watch the ship with none the wiser."

Aggarwal chimed in. "If the Trads agree."

"They will," said the man in gray. He leaned back as if he had no more to say.

"The alien ship is as much a threat to them as it is to us," Rubik added.

Neville looked unconvinced. He peered down his nose at Leclerc. "You're certain it's coming to Sol system, and not a star that happens to lie behind us on the same line of travel?"

"We're certain. There's no star on that line for hundreds of light-years."

"And it's coming how quickly?"

"Our best calculations show it's been accelerating at a constant 1.1993 *gee* since its engine burn."

"For simplicity, we'll round it to 1.2 *gee*," said Rubik. "Why that acceleration?"

"We surmise that is the surface gravity of the aliens' homeworld."

She glanced to her side. Her fingers slid through air. "More confirmation they aren't from Four Freedoms."

Neville cleared his throat. "I would rather Mr. Leclerc opine on that."

Leclerc wanted to pat his bald scalp, but kept his hand at his side. *And don't call the planet Bravo Charlie.* "Four Freedoms has a surface gravity of about 0.8 *gee*. Much lower than the ship's acceleration. We assume any aliens would choose the same default we did with *Concordia*, and accelerate at the surface gravity of their home-world. For crew comfort."

"Mightn't they accelerate faster than their surface gravity to throw us off the scent of their origins?" asked Neville.

A snort from near the window. "Looks to me the ship's coming from Four Freedoms." Memford leaned back, squeaking his chair. "Though they might boost harder because they know we can see them coming. To get here faster."

"Assuming a brachistochrone trajectory—constant acceleration to the halfway point, then constant deceleration the rest of the way," Leclerc said, "the alien ship's flight time in our reference frame would be about five years and two months."

Neville let out a breath. "A great deal of time before it arrives."

Leclerc's throat tightened. He glanced at Aggarwal, then Rubik, but both leaned away from him. They left him the hard job of explaining to Neville.

"Pardon me, I must have misspoken. That's five years and two months from when it launched. Four years and four months ago."

Neville's waved a lazy hand. "Oh, yes, light speed, relativity. It's been a long time since I've used my advanced maths." His eyes tracked to the ceiling behind Leclerc and his head bobbed, as if he did the math in his mind and confirmed the right answer at each step. His eyebrows arched. "They'll be here in ten months."

Memford spoke, sarcasm temporarily forgotten. "Assuming it runs a brak—a burn and turn trajectory."

"A safe assumption," Leclerc said. "They have so much energy available, they have no need to coast to save fuel."

"Ten months," said Rubik. "Till arrival."

"Merry Christmas," Memford said, then chuckled to himself.

CHAPTER 9

7 MARCH 2132

THE SLANT of the room's timbers suddenly seemed at a greater angle, as if the chamber, as if all of Cheltenford Hall, had its foundations knocked out and teetered at collapse.

"The 16th of December, to be exact," Leclerc said. Regret panged him. The exact date wasn't important, in the face of the hush settling over the room. Though natural gas flames hissed in the fireplace and warm dry air rumbled out of the vents, a chill smothered Leclerc's arms.

Rubik gave Leclerc a probing look with her blue eyes. "Is the date it arrives. Won't it become visible before that?"

Sharp question. "To the naked eye? Or to amateurs with backyard telescopes?"

"Both."

"After turnover, it will decelerate toward us with the same power it accelerates now. We'll see the exhaust beam head on."

"Turnover would be visible in five months? Early August?" She absently fingered her cravat.

"The light would reach us in the last week of July. But turnover would not be immediately apparent. The two stars of Alpha Centauri, particularly B, will backlight the ship's exhaust."

Memford ran a finger from his eye toward Leclerc's. "Same line of sight," he said, sarcasm set aside for the moment.

"At first, it will appear Alpha Centauri B is brightening. A university or science agency telescope could resolve the ship's exhaust beam against the stars within a month or so after turnover."

"By September," Rubik said.

Wistful regret washed through Leclerc. August, lounging next to Sybil on a tropical beach. God willing he still could take his vacation this year.

God knew what vacations, if any, he could take after the aliens came.

Leclerc refocused on the moment. "Even if we cover up data gathered from professional astronomers, backyard stargazers would still see it by November. Anyone out at night will see it with the naked eye in December."

Memford stretched his arms behind his head. The rock band logo T-shirt slid up his chest. "For latitudes that can see it. Europe and most of North America are too far north."

"You cannot quarantine the information," said Rubik. "Word will spread."

"I hear where you're coming from," Aggarwal said in a lapdog voice to Memford. "But maybe we shouldn't, like, assume the Trads would keep it hidden too."

Neville peered down his long nose. "They will. They want to maintain their iron grip on the minds of their subjects." Hands on the tabletop, he intertwined his fingers. "We've established an alien ship is coming to Earth. Its approach will be noticeable by November and it will arrive in mid-December. What are its intentions?"

Memford scratched his shoulder through the black T-shirt. "Perhaps they come in peace."

Neville turned his way. "You seem to believe they have hostile intentions."

"They could have been listening to us for a couple hundred years. If they were just going to say howdy to the neighbors, they would have transmitted something decades ago. If they wanted to make a friendly visit, why wait till now? Why wait till we show we can travel near light speed and cross interstellar distances? When we show we're near peers, and thus a threat?"

"Trade at interstellar distances is impossibly expensive," Rubik said. "All economists agree."

The gray man shifted his weight enough to be noticed. "They don't need to trade." He waited till eyes turned his way. "If they can harness the energy to use light as reaction mass, they have enough energy to find and purify any natural atom, transmute any artificial one, and combine them to make anything they need."

Rubik broke the ensuing silence. "We're all agreed. They do not come to trade."

"Mightn't they have a spirit of exploration?" Neville asked. "Like us?"

"What motivated the explorations of human history?" The gray man worked his mouth for a moment, as if speaking so much tired his jaw. "Money and power, with sex in third place."

"We've ruled out money," said Rubik.

Memford chuckled. "Maybe they want to star in some tentacle porn."

Neville squinted at the sarcastic American. "I don't follow."

"Does anyone here get turned on by nature documentaries about birds, reptiles, or insects mating? We'd look even less sexy to aliens than that. Which only leaves one thing."

"Power," murmured Rubik.

Memford put on a cowboy accent. "'This here galaxy ain't big enough for the two of us.'"

"They come to fight." Rubik hugger her arms through her sea-green blouse.

"We hope," muttered Evans. Loudly enough for Leclerc to suck in a breath.

Rubik turned her blue eyes on Leclerc. "You and your people want to fight aliens with powers a thousand-fold greater than ours?"

Leclerc tightened his lips and glared at Evans. Evans bowed his head, apology in the slump of his shoulders.

Leclerc's heart slowed from a gallop. Not Evans' fault. The power brokers needed to know about the worst case.

"We don't want to fight them, but there is something worse than that."

Rubik canted her head. The angle made it seem her beehive hairdo could slide off. "What could be worse?"

Leclerc managed a dry swallow. "Annihilation."

"How?"

"The simplest way for them to do so would be a suicide mission. If the alien ship accelerated non-stop, and ran into the sun at over 0.99 c, the resulting explosion would look like a nova."

The blonde fingered the knot in her orange cravat. "Earth wouldn't stand a chance."

Memford scrunched up his lean face. "They might be aliens, but they wouldn't launch a suicide mission. Evolution would give them the same self-preservation instinct it gave us." He shook his head and leaned back to stare out the window, point made.

Leclerc craved such certainty. He'd lain awake at night, cold sweat on his forehead, immobile as a dead man for fear of waking Sybil and having to compound his lies of omission to her. She didn't even know about the alien presence on Bravo Charlie. Let alone its departure for Earth.

"I agree it seems unlikely any conscious mind could choose a suicide mission." Leclerc grimaced. "But they may have programmed a robotic ship to do so."

The people behind the table gave little shakes of their heads. If you wielded great power, first you used it to bend others to your will. Only if that failed would you consider annihilation. Such was the twisted morality of their arena. And you wouldn't hand a machine the keys to your doomsday weapon.

Facts, too, suggested the alien ship probably did not come to annihilate Earth. Though *Concordia*'s radio silence continued, and Leclerc doubted the human ship would ever restore contact, the scope array sometimes glimpsed it in orbit. The terrain under the human science bases on Bravo Charlie had not been melted to bedrock. If the aliens were active in the galaxy and had genocide on their minds, they would long ago have detected humankind's radio transmissions, found Earth, and destroyed it.

Following that line of reasoning, he'd fallen back asleep. But he could only rule out the extermination option if the alien ship reached the halfway point and decelerated.

"We do appreciate you considered all the possibilities," Neville said. He glanced at Evans as if noticing him for the first time, then returned his attention to Leclerc and Aggarwal. "Assume they stop in the solar system with ill intent. What might they do? And how could we counter it?"

Aggarwal angled his head from side to side. "I think Leclerc can explain it better." A flat look showed he wanted to make Leclerc the bearer of bad news.

Someone had to. Leclerc said, "From Earth orbit, they could strike essentially any target on the surface. With high-speed kinetic impactors—"

"The old 'rods from God' idea," Memford said.

"Yes. Though directed energy weapons seem more likely. With as much power as they must be using to fly their ship, they could spare a tiny amount for a laser that could vaporize a city. Finally, they could use the exhaust beam as a weapon. Far more energy than a laser, but less focus."

"We could defend against energy weapons by....?" Neville glanced from side to side.

"Dispersing," said Aggarwal. "Going underground."

"We should have time for that," said Rubik. "They won't know the location of Alliance headquarters or any Humanist member capital. They'll need to gather intel. Presumably from signals intelligence—"

"No way they have any humint." Memford's sarcasm returned.

Rubik swung her head his way. "How would they have gained human intelligence?"

"Taking prisoners. There were six people poking around the ship's hiding place, remember? The aliens or their robots or whatever have had five years to torture them."

Leclerc's lips parted. With time dilation, the alien ship's journey would take closer to three.

He shut his mouth. Weeds. Three years or five, enough time to torture human captives. Or for captives to talk of their own free will. Hit these Trad targets. Or these Humanist ones.

Or a plague on both their houses...

Yet intel or not.... "While we could harden official functions, the aliens might target cities."

Rubik gave a faint smile. "We'll take care of civil defense when the time comes."

Neville cleared his throat and sat taller. "People will keep calm and carry on. Protecting ourselves is well and good. It is not enough. How will we strike back?"

For a moment, only the hiss of the natural gas fireplace sounded in the room. Then Aggarwal chimed in, eager to please. "Nukes."

Memford leaned back and folded his arms across the rock band logo. He rocked enough to make his chair squeak. "Thinking big. I like that."

The man in gray said, "Bad idea."

"And I thought you had a pair, Osorio." Memford laughed.

Pair? Leclerc wondered. Ah, of testicles. Some American cowboy idiom.

How calm and reasoned the debates within the Humanist Alliance's inner sanctum.

"Yes, I have a pair. Of reasons." Osorio raised his gray sleeve and jutted out stubby fingers as he made his points in his faint Latin accent. "One. The main destructive power of a nuclear weapon on a planet comes from the atmospheric shock wave. This does not exist in vacuum."

Memford put on a lazy smirk. "I could've sworn radiation output would be the same either place."

"An interstellar ship would have shielding against relativistic cosmic rays. The same would blunt a nuclear weapon's radiation burst. Two. Detonating a nuclear weapon in orbit would cause an electromagnetic pulse to knock out power and computers over millions of square kilometers."

Destroying infrastructure for billions of people. A humanitarian disaster to dwarf the world wars of the twentieth century, or the Chinese hegemony of the twenty-first. Even if it somehow destroyed a hostile alien ship in the process, it would be a cure worse than the disease.

Leclerc's blood ran cold. He scanned the faces across the table. Did they actually contemplate a continent-wrecking EMP as a price worth paying?

Worse. As a price worth billions of common people paying, while these elites hid underground, supported by shielded computers and other systems?

A thought came to him, Aggarwal's admonition be damned. "We could build our own energy weapons," he blurted.

Silence reigned. Aggarwal broke it. His voice sounded mild. "Yeah we talked about coming in."

Leclerc gritted his teeth. Aggarwal lied to take credit, and he had no way of telling the power brokers behind the table the truth.

"Like, this is important. Don't leave them hanging."

Leclerc took a breath. He didn't need credit if the Earth could defend itself from an alien threat. "For example, we have ground-based lasers to blind satellites."

Osorio nodded. At least one person behind the table knew the unsung key to the Humanist-Traditionalist joint victory over the Chinese.

"Are those lasers powerful enough?" Rubik mused.

Memford rubbed his knuckles on the rock band logo. "The aliens could line up ground installations like ducks in a shooting gallery."

Leclerc hurried on. "Make them mobile. Airplanes. Oceangoing ships. Submarines. Or a combination."

Memford picked up a stylus from the table in front of him and twirled it in his fingers. Then he dropped it in disgust. "Submarines would have to surface to fire."

The man in gray, Osorio, spoke. "Then submerge immediately after. Shielded by billions of tons of seawater."

"And we can lose a few if we build a large enough fleet," said Rubik.

"Of submarines capable of sneaking into a Trad harbor and leveling a city?" Memford snorted. "They'll sign on to that in a heartbeat."

Leclerc spoke up, his voice coming out of a dry mouth. "Perhaps they would agree if we build it with them."

Silence fell over the room. Neville arched an eyebrow. Memford smirked at Leclerc like a cat might at a mouse. Aggarwal shifted over and slapped a hand down on Leclerc's shoulder. He spoke through a feigned smile. "We're done talking, you know, about the science of the alien ship."

The threat came through. Leclerc shuffled back a step.

Memford's cold laugh came from near the window. "Commissar Guo got to you, huh?"

Leclerc dropped his gaze to the herringbone parquet. His cheeks felt hot.

"She played you, Leclerc," said Memford. "I thought you Frenchies were wise to women's tricks."

With an icy gaze at Memford from under her lofted hair, Rubik looked like a haughty queen from before the Revolution.

"Leclerc's got a point," said Osorio.

Memford whipped his head around. "She got to you too?"

The man's dark eyes flickered over Memford once, then away. "If the aliens come to Earth with hostile intent, will they care about Humanist or Traditionalist?"

Neville squinted down his long nose. "You propose we work with the Trads? Our only enemies?"

"We worked with them half a century ago to defeat the Chinese."

"And in the aftermath of victory," Neville said, "they attempted to become world hegemons in their place."

A silence of tight smiles broke when Rubik chuckled. Enough to break the ice for the others flanking Neville to laugh as well.

Neville looked sheepish, but only for a moment. "Yes, we tried the same." He raised an eyebrow at Leclerc and Evans, mirth in his face. Let's conspire together to keep the truth hidden, whilst telling the Humanist masses our anti-Trad pious lies. "The point remains. How can we work with them?"

The bands of power slicing through the room hemmed Leclerc in. Aggarwal shifted his weight enough to remind him of the warning given in the parking lot.

But an alien ship, likely with hostile intent, was less than a year away. Their political infighting and internal status games were not worth a damn.

"Perhaps even now the Traditionalists are asking themselves the same question," he said.

Aggarwal cleared his throat, loud and harsh.

Leclerc straightened his neck. Sweat ran down his nape. "As Mr. Osorio said—" He bowed to the man in the gray suit. "—will the aliens care about one faction or the other? The Traditionalists would no longer be our only enemies, if the aliens come to do violence against Earth."

Osorio gave a ponderous nod of his head. "I see I'm not the only sensible person in the room."

Next to him, Rubik looked down the table. Her gaze met Memford's. The two shared some message in the glance Leclerc could not decode.

She leaned back and brushed lint of her blouse sleeve. The American aimed his hatchet face at Osorio. "The Trads will chimp out if we build a fleet of submarines we can turn against their cities."

"We build the fleet together. Deploy it together. A joint service. Officers from both sides in each boat's control room."

Memford made a *plff* sound, blowing out his cheeks with mouth half-open.

Rubik tilted her beehive left and right. It rose straight up when she spoke. "I see the merit in a joint venture. Pooling resources and specializing in our comparative advantages would allow us to build a stronger defense."

"They have better shipbuilding facilities than us," said Osorio. "Which would pair well with our advances in high energy lasers."

"But how do we build trust with them?" said Neville.

Memford smirked. "Leclerc has a rapport with Commissar Guo. Let him do it."

The room suddenly seemed hotter. Leclerc froze. "I'm flattered. But my talents best serve the Humanist Alliance in my post at mission control."

With a lazy wave and smile, Memford said, "The graveyards are full of indispensable men. Evans, can you handle mission control? And Hagerty?"

Evans's lanky limbs squirmed. "If I must." The wince on his tanned face sounded in his voice. "I learned from the best."

"Leclerc's very strong on the technical side." Aggarwal spoke eagerly. "But he can't do it alone. Guo's feminine wiles, am I right?"

Rubik gave Leclerc a condescending smile. "His mind and heart are in the right place. But his other parts...?"

Warmth flushed Leclerc's cheeks. "I've ever been faithful to my wife—"

"Sybil. Yes, we know you have never dallied." Rubik's blue eyes looked as cold as turquoise on black velvet. "But you would swim in deeper waters than you ever have before. Aggarwal would make an adequate lifeguard."

From near the window came a snort. "You're serious," said Memford.

She plastered on a smile. "You proposed an excellent idea."

Leclerc swallowed and shuffled back a step. Rubik and Memford were giant creatures of the ocean deeps, locked in a struggle that would crush a mere human diver unnoticed between them. Whatever chains of political and personal history lay between them, he desperately wanted to stay unsnared from them.

From all of them behind the table. He wanted to go home, to deal with scientists and not shadowy figures with vast yet hidden powers. To process the backlog of data from *Concordia* by day. To sleep next to his wife by night.

In the video, the right edge of the window clipped the ring of light.

He wasn't going to get back to his comfortable life for another ten months. Or more.

In the center of the table, Neville cleared his throat. "I'll take the following proposal to the high council. A joint venture with the Trads to build and deploy a fleet of laser submarines, for defense against the alien ship. With Leclerc as our chief scientific liaison to them, guided by Aggarwal. Agreed?"

Rubik said, "Yes." Osorio lifted a finger. Memford stared out the window.

"Agreed." Neville peered down his nose at Leclerc. "Congratulations," he said, voice laced with irony.

Aggarwal chimed in. "Like, you won't regret it."

"We'll hold you to that," Neville said.

Leclerc suddenly felt chill. The cold feeling dogged him as the meeting broke up. Past the natural gas fireplaces and brocaded curtains on the way out of the country house. All the way back home.

CHAPTER 10

17 MAY 2130 (EARTH REFERENCE FRAME) | 19 JULY 2127 (*NAPOLEON* REFERENCE FRAME)

JAEGER'S EARS had long ago tuned out the quiet droning note of the Octalien ship's drive. When the engines stopped their constant acceleration, the silence ringing in his ears added to his stomach flopping in free-fall, and a mix of antsiness and weariness flowing down his limbs.

Halfway to Earth.

Still over eighteen months to go.

He took a ragged breath. One thing at a time.

He and Ulanovas crowded into the control room. Built for Octaliens, and not many at once. Jaeger floated, acutely conscious of the equipment they'd fabricated and hacked into place. The control room felt like a closet at an electronics testing lab. The air smelled of soap and Ulanovas's sandy-blond hair, usually feathery, lay flat and damp on his head.

Jaeger's hunched shoulders bumped the low ceiling. "Ready?"

"A moment." Ulanovas gestured at a video monitor, stuck on the front wall, wedged under the ceiling. "This is our last clean look at Sol system until we stop, okay?"

Jaeger raised his eyebrows at the monitor. "Not much to see."

"It's the principle, okay?"

Okay. A blue-white spot, like a welder's torch, blazed among the tinier, dimmer pinpoints of the constellation Cassiopeia, and ten thousand stars more distant. A faint, flickering sheen, arising the ship's thick cap of rock plowed into interstellar hydrogen atoms, veiled the actinic points but could not blunt them.

The blue-white spot was Sol. Their immense velocity, north of 0.99 c, Doppler-shifted Sol's light so far up the spectrum that green dots glowed in Jaeger's vision when he blinked his eyes.

But the sun only. Earth and the other planets were still too small to be seen.

"Prepare to maneuver," Jaeger said.

"Aye aye, captain." It always sounded like Ulanovas joked when he spoke like a sailor in a movie, but from time to time Jaeger wondered if some sharper edge hid behind his tone. Over a year and a half in a tin can was getting to them all.

How much worse would it get over the next five years?

The Lithuanian jammed his bent legs against back wall, his left arm against the front one, and moved his right hand to a control board they'd added. "Ready."

"Yaw delta one-eighty."

"Yawing now." Ulanovas tapped keys like a stenographer, chording combinations so quickly Jaeger couldn't follow.

Yes, the rest of them could fly the ship. In theory. But in practice, if some bad fate befell Ulanovas....

For all the ship's immense power, its attitude controls were barely more advanced than *Concordia*'s. *Napoleon* jetted out streams of hydrogen remass gathered from interstellar space. They'd gathered the hydrogen using a miniature version of *Concordia*'s particle spin magnets. The pinnacle of human propulsion technology, scaled down and used by the Octaliens as an afterthought.

Still, it would take fifteen minutes to get the ship into the proper orientation, bass-ackward to Earth.

"Ceasing active," Ulanovas said.

Jaeger couldn't feel the difference. They were too near the ship's central axis, and the vessel moved too slowly. Nowhere near enough spin gravity to keep his stomach happy.

Numbers on a display showed a steady change in the ship's orientation in x, y, and z planes relative to the galactic ecliptic. But it wasn't until Sol slid off the forward camera view, and the unnamed stars seen in its place forward camera changed from blinding blue-white to normal shades, that the knowledge went from his head into his body.

Halfway through the turn.

A slimy feeling sloshed around Jaeger's gut. The same interstellar hydrogen atoms generating a flickering sheen when they impacted the rock cap were now blasting the sides of the cylindrical ship.

The hull should handle it. They'd send out robots to inspect and repair if needed, after the deceleration burn started. But if even a microgram particle of dust drifted across their path at their current speed, it could punch a hole in the hull too big for the robots to repair.

Or worse.

Bile crawled up his throat. Even if he took another anti-nausea pill now, it would kick in too late to do any good. The stars in the fore view now looked shrunken and red as drops of drying blood. Like the whole Universe was dying.

Jaeger took a deep breath. No need for maudlin thoughts. The stars looked red thanks to more Doppler shift. A trick of how their light looked, chasing a ship fleeing them a hair below lightspeed.

"Prepping active retro yaw... now." Ulanovas tapped out another sequence of keys.

Jaeger still couldn't feel it, but the x, y, and z numbers slowed their changes, and the ponderous scrolling of the redshifted stars wheezed to a halt.

"Switch to aft cam—"

The familiar blue-white glow of Sol amid Cassiopeia returned. Streaks flashed through the flickering veil of interstellar hydrogen impacts. Not worse than before, just different, hitting Octalien alloy instead of the cap of rock.

"We're lined up?" Jaeger asked.

"Yes," Ulanovas said, mildly exasperated. He muttered something in Lithuanian. Jaeger picked out enough to tell he gave voice commands to his wearable computer. "Look at the delta in the orientation numbers, okay?"

Jaeger's wearable received the data push and popped it into his vision. Sets of numbers and a 3d graph. A straight line across interstellar space, solid going back to Alpha Centauri, dashed continuing along their path. He extended his hand and rotated the graph. Straight as an arrow from every perspective.

A brighter streak than usual pulled his eye back to the main screen. Stop wasting time. He opened a channel to the rest of the team. "Prepare for burn. McIlroy? Marie?"

Their *roger* and *check* echoed in each other's microphones.

"Annike?"

"I wish we could coast a while longer." Her reserved voice had a wistful tone.

"I hear you," Jaeger said despite the unease in his stomach. Though she agreed with the camouflage and shorter travel time provided by their high acceleration, she continually grumbled about the 1.2 *gee*. "But we have to—"

"I know."

Jaeger paused before speaking. "Six second ramp up will start in five. Four...."

He and Ulanovas backed against the rear wall. Jaeger folded his creaky knees. Not to meditate, but to keep from bumping his legs into controls when thrust-gravity returned. With one hand, he reached up to the ceiling, then moved his other to the engine control panel. "Two. One. Burn begins."

He nudged the acceleration slider forward. His rump and the backs of his thighs settled to the floor. Despite his legs's lotus position, his right knee clipped an edge of an original Octalien control board. He winced and rubbed it with his free hand.

Thrust-gravity crept up. Point-eight *gee*, comfortable as Bravo Charlie's surface. One-point-oh, like the Earth he might never again walk upon.

The slider jammed against the far end of its track. One-point-two *gee*. Meant to get them to Earth a couple of months faster. Meant to look alien. Acceptable risks on middle-aged hearts.

"Burn full." Jaeger swung the clear cover down over the slider, then locked it. He unfolded his knees and crawled out of the control room. Ulanovas followed.

Both stood up in the twisty corridor outside. Jaeger's stomach settled. His anxious mood faded. They'd survived the risks of turnover. A blaze of light shielded them now and for the rest of the journey. He stretched arms sculpted from daily life at 1.2 *gee*. Toned muscles were one of the pluses of *Napoleon*'s constant high thrust, but an ache in his left knee reminded him of the minuses.

The wear and tear on their bodies would be worth it, if they scared the Traditionalist and Humanist leaderships into cooperating against the "alien" threat.

A dark flicker crossed his mood.

If.

CHAPTER 11

24 JULY 2132

Leclerc kept the blackout curtains closed day and night. By day to avoid seeing the bleak city outside, of low roofs and low skies, of the cranes and drydocks of the shipyard, of maples whose intense green leaves emphasized the fleeting shortness of the summer. By night to block the midnight twilight and the full sunlight of three a.m.

But despite the curtains and his sleep mask, he tossed and turned on the memory foam bed. He'd given orders, to Evans and the rest of the team at mission control, to alert him as soon as they saw the alien ship turn over. Any time, day or night.

He kicked his legs free of the blanket. Sweat crawled through what remained of his hair. They'd run the numbers twice. The bright exhaust of the alien ship decelerating should have reached Earth hours ago.

Unless the ship hadn't turned over. Unless a robotic crew planned a suicide mission to obliterate Sol system.

He shivered. He groped for the blanket, grabbed it. A fold, not the edge. He pulled it over but couldn't cover himself fully.

A sigh, then he raised his sleep mask. Slivers of daylight showed around the blackout curtain. He sat up. A glimpse of the antique wooden desk in the corner and the extruded television bolted to the wall. He unfolded the blanket, lay back down under its warmth. The odor of stale sheets clogged his nose. Call housekeeping in the morning for a change of linens.

He reached for his sleep mask but his hand suddenly felt too heavy to pull it over his eyes. Would clean sheets matter?

Why hadn't mission control called?

A chime sounded in his earbuds, then repeated. An icon flashed in a corner of his vision, superimposed on the ceiling near a strip of light. A black telephone, an ancient wired kind. The handset danced in its cradle in sync with the chime. Under the icon appeared the words *Wojniakowski, IIEA HQ*.

He reached up and poked the icon with his fingertip.

A video window opened on the ceiling. Woj and Yasmina Khan filled the center of the screen, with the ledge around the horseshoe visible to the sides. Khan wore a mint-green headscarf with wisps of hair sneaking out the front. The stuffed chimera's four splayed legs flopped on the ledge. In the background, the main screen showed the circle of Bravo Charlie. Green and sunlit coast drew Leclerc's eye. A tooltip pointed at an infinitesimal point at the shore, Glenn Station, the last known whereabouts of three dozen scientists.

Homesickness panged Leclerc. Would that he could be at mission control again, expanding the frontiers of knowledge. "Good morning," he said. Audio only.

Woj had grown out his brown hair and held it out of his eyes with a white sweatband. A better hairstyle than he'd sported last winter. He also sported a stubbly beard. "Good morning, sir. It's morning, yes? You're only two hours ahead?"

"I believe only one during the summer." Leclerc could look it up, but didn't want to. Knowing the details of time zones and daylight saving laws would make it feel like he belonged in this dour industrial town in arctic Russia.

Woj looked aside at something virtual. "So you know, Khan brought Dr. Guo on the line as well."

"Fine." Leclerc yawned. "Good morning to you also, Doctor." He saw her daily around the shipyard, but after hours, she went to a different hotel here in Severodvinsk. Probably one without Russian and Coalition counterintelligence personnel watching her every move.

"I see you asked for a wake up call also," she said. Her disembodied voice came from his left. "I take it the ship turned over?"

"Yes," said Khan. Relief showed in her brown eyes and on her rouged lips.

Leclerc let out a breath. The doomsday scenario looked unlikely, and would grow more so with every second the alien ship decelerated.

Woj added, "We'll put the video on the main screen." He looked over his shoulder and spoke to someone seated behind him and Khan.

Keys clacked. A brightly colored wheel spun over the planet's terminator line between day and night.

The wheel vanished and the image behind it changed in a blink. A dot of piercing blue-white blazed against the yellow and orange of Alpha Centauri A and B behind it, and the soft backdrop of ten thousand other stars. A popup window showed spectral analysis of the dot. The same beam of pure light glimpsed back in March, but crowded to shorter wavelengths by a velocity a tiny fraction below lightspeed.

"Deceleration rate and vector?" Leclerc asked.

"The same as its boost phase," said Khan. "Slightly under 1.1993 *gee*. On course for Sol system. Expected arrival remains December 16."

His wearable adjusted Guo's voice to make it seem she spoke to him. "Our work is not in vain."

"Indeed," Leclerc said. He breathed deeply, never mind the stale scent of unchanged sheets. "Woj, Khan, do you have more?"

"No, sir. If it deviates from its current trajectory, or does something unexpected, we'll let you know."

A long slow whisper, Guo drawing a breath. "Has it transmitted any messages?"

"No, Doctor." Woj mashed his lips together.

No sign of the ship's intent. No basis to assume it came in peace. All they had to go on were the facts of a ship more powerful than long-muted *Concordia*, flown by minds with no need to trade. "Our work remains necessary," Leclerc said.

Guo's gentle voice chided him. "It would remain necessary even if it announced it came in peace. One must prepare based on capabilities, not words." Her voice changed tone. He pictured a faint smile on her lips. "But we have time enough to resume our preparations in the morning. Till then." She left the call. Woj and Khan soon followed.

Leclerc pulled down his sleep mask, but tossed and turned as much as he had before.

Time enough? Less than five months till the ship itself arrived.

The sun, low in the southeastern sky, cast their long shadows across the patched asphalt of the parking lot. Leclerc trudged next to Aggarwal. The aides assigned to them by the Russian authorities kept pace, the brunette with the downturned mouth ahead and the young man with the broad cheekbones behind. *Aides*, true enough, translators and gofers. But undoubtedly counterintelligence as well.

The vast concrete drydock building loomed ahead of them, blocking the view of low clouds to the north above the frigid ocean. The tiny windows near one upper corner of the drydock, where the offices were, always looked like a prisoner might flash a *help me* sign in faint hope of being rescued.

The brunette halted at a pedestrian gate in the middle of a barbed wire fence. A coil of more barbed wire leaned outward from the top. Two guards in Russian naval uniforms stalked from under their awnings on either side of the gate. Their slung automatic weapons bounced against their shoulder blades with each step.

She spoke in Russian to the guard with the East Asian cast to his brown eyes. He gave her a smile as he replied.

The other guard, who had eyes like blue ice in deep sockets, did not smile or speak. He beckoned for Aggarwal and Leclerc to lift their badges from their belts. Leclerc tugged his up. The reel connecting badge to holder unwound wire with a screeing sound.

Icy eyes looked from badge photos to faces. The guard brought from inside his jacket a gray plastic box slightly bigger than his hand. Leclerc didn't need to read the Cyrillic on the sides to know it was a portable DNA sequencer.

The guard flipped open the cover on one port and nodded at Aggarwal. Bushy eyebrows knotted. "Like, why do we always do this charade?"

Leclerc sighed. Yes, the same guards worked here five days a week and knew them by sight, but what good could come of arguing?

Aggarwal stuck his middle finger in the port. Leclerc assumed the guard knew Aggarwal made an obscene gesture, but the cold blue eyes showed no offense. Though was that a hint of a smile when Aggarwal sniffed out a breath, and again when he shook his finger after freeing it from the machine?

Leclerc inserted his index finger and held his hand steady. A tiny prick when the sterile needle drew blood, followed by a cool drop of topical analgesic and liquid bandage. He pulled out his finger. He couldn't see where the needle had pierced his skin.

The guard peered at the back of the unit. A video screen, Leclerc knew, but he couldn't see it, let alone read it. Leclerc stood there, shifting his weight in the cold offshore wind. The clouds crept closer. By afternoon it would likely rain. The brunette and the Asiatic guard chatted as if it were a balmy day.

For them, it was. Poor souls. Leclerc inwardly cursed that no tropical beach waited for him next month. At least Sybil waited at home, and knew why he'd been sent here, and would keep the reason why a secret.

The DNA sequencer bonged a couple of times. The guard's blue eyes scanned lines of text on its screen. He stepped back with a crack of boot soles on the asphalt.

The Asiatic guard gave the brunette a last smile, then beckoned the party through.

Another broad paved plaza, this one for delivery trucks. Ahead, the drydock's door for foot traffic looked like a mouse hole. The building's gargantuan, inhuman proportions carried into the interior. Three football pitches long, two wide, one high. The docks proper took up most of the floor space. The air was as cool as the so-called summer day outside, though the thick walls kept out the wind.

The brunette led the way between the outer wall and the nearer dock's pumped-dry pit. A thin handrail, striped yellow and black and the length of the pit, seemed too flimsy a protection between the walkway and the ten-meter drop.

In the docks, two submarines squatted on arrays of hydraulic jacks. Sparks danced around the midsection of the far one, where a ceiling-mounted crane held a curved slab of metal for workers to weld to the boat's half-exposed ribs. More workmen clambered over the near submarine, magnetic boots and iron nerves keeping them atop it. Three of them, standing around an open hatch originally designed for the launch of intercontinental missiles, stopped to regard Leclerc and Aggarwal through wary eyes. They muttered to themselves, their Russian words half-masked by the clang and grunt of equipment.

Leclerc guessed at what they spoke of. *Why do they need launch bays for a submarine to explore an alien ocean?*

It pleased him slightly, to know that soon the men working so hard in this place could learn why.

The brunette led the way up open metal stairs bolted onto the building's outer wall. Leclerc kept one hand on the railing and his eyes on their destination. The metal rang arrhythmically from all their steps. Though the brunette's jeans emphasized her shapely legs, his gaze did not linger. From love for Sybil, mingled with dread of all the stories of men trapped in a honeypot by foreign intelligence and blackmailed into espionage.

Even if they worked together to defend Earth, how long would the gap between factions and nations remain?

The office suite bulged from the building's corner like a rectilinear lump in someone's armpit. No guards, but a steel door at the top of the stairs only opened when the brunette scanned her badge. She led the way through a cubicle farm under artificial light. Chatter and the rustle of bodies in seats halted. The clerical staff all stared straight ahead, not even glancing Leclerc and Aggarwal's way as the Humanists and their guides crossed the space.

She stopped at a door. The glow of daylight came through the frosted glass pane, silhouetting the Cyrillic lettering. Leclerc's wearable overlaid a translation, though he no longer needed it to know the occupant's name and title. *C. Orlovsky, Director of Operations.*

The brunette waved her hand over a scanner mounted on the wall. A grunt of *"Da"* came from inside, followed by a low thud as the door's electromagnetic lock unsealed.

In they went. Only as the young male aide swung shut the door behind them did the clerical staffers let out their breaths and get back to work.

Orlovsky sat behind an L-shaped desk, backlit by the summer sun through the room's only window. Creased face, cropped hair slicked down, short but wiry stature, he'd given a few hints of having served on Russian submarines similar to the ones being refurbished in the pit before moving into his current role. Though he wore an ill-fitting dress shirt and a patched jacket instead of a naval uniform, Leclerc kept thinking of him as active duty.

Seated on the other side of the short arm of the desk, tucked in a corner of the room between a bookcase and a print of a surfaced submarine, sat Guo. She'd traded the floral print dress for a skirt suit in navy blue. Her jade and porcelain pendant rested against a pastel blue blouse. She bowed her head a fraction in greeting.

Orlovsky gestured at a pair of empty chairs in front of the other leg of his desk, and spoke. "Sit, please," the young male aide translated.

Leclerc waited for Aggarwal to pick a seat. The bureaucrat chose the one closest to Guo and crossed his legs, right ankle up, right knee aimed at her.

He grimaced slightly. Aggarwal still harbored a grudge over Guo's impromptu alliance with him in mission control back in January. Leclerc covered his grimace and took the remaining seat.

"Dr. Guo tells me aliens will stop at Earth," Orlovsky said through the translator.

"We read the data the same way," said Leclerc. "Turnover when we predicted, and deceleration at the same rate as acceleration. It should enter Earth orbit in about four and a half months."

The lines on Orlovsky's face deepened. "Yes, you have said this. But you do not act urgent."

Leclerc frowned. Aggarwal jumped in. "Like, what do you mean? We've been here for weeks offering all the help you need—"

"You are laser engineers? No." Orlovsky folded his arms and scowled.

Guo spoke calmly. Plainly, the two Trads had worked out the bad cop-good cop routine before Leclerc and Aggarwal arrived. "We have done all that our factions negotiated, according to the agreed timeline. Two submarines, built to modified ballistic missile specifications, one to be completed today and one by August 1. You saw them as you entered." The brunette translated for Orlovsky, her voice a lilting murmur that forced Leclerc to concentrate on Guo's words.

"Yes," Leclerc said. Aggarwal studied the heel of his right shoe.

"The agreement called for Humanist personnel at Lawrence Livermore laboratory, in California, to make ready four laser cannons by now. Two per boat."

Aggarwal jerked his head side-to-side. "Ready doesn't mean delivered."

"True. It means in condition to be delivered. But according to your people, they are undergoing additional quality assurance testing. Why would this be?"

Orlovsky grunted out some words. "Is always when West and Russia are allies. Russia does most fighting. And most dying."

Leclerc spread his palms. "I hear your concern. But this is not a repeat of 1941. Or 1812. Our lands are as exposed to the sky as yours. The hostile power coming toward us has forces far greater than the Wehrmacht or the Grande Armée. Forces which cannot be fatally weakened in an attack on Russia. The best chance for both our factions to survive is by working together."

Mildly, Aggarwal said, "The delay coming out of Lawrence Livermore is, like, technical. That's what they tell me, you know? Maybe Leclerc and I should fly out there. See for ourselves."

A warm spot grew in Leclerc's chest. It wouldn't be a tropical beach, and Sybil couldn't join him, but dry air and sunny skies pulled him like a magnet. Humanist counterintel at the former American national laboratory was far more subtle than here, and would barely glance over him.

In the window behind Orlovsky, clouds bunched up toward the sun. "They will blame us for delay," he said to Guo. "Claim we give faulty specifications."

Guo extended her slender arm over the desk toward him. "I will travel with them. They would be unable to lie."

Leclerc tensed and glanced at Aggarwal.

The bureaucrat smiled, though the expression didn't reach his eyes. "That's a great idea. You know, to get rid of misunderstandings."

What trick did he play?

Leclerc smoothed down what remained of his hair. Why assume the worst about the science bureaucrat? Perhaps Aggarwal finally realized they only had a few months to prepare for aliens carrying more firepower than all the armies of human history combined.

Orlovsky asked Guo a cautious question. "Coalition headquarters will approve?"

"I'm not needed here. You've done excellent work and that won't change. Yes?"

Orlovsky sat up straighter. "*Da.*"

"It's settled." Guo gave Leclerc and Aggarwal a faint smile. "Can the two of you leave on the afternoon flight?"

They changed planes in Moscow, then again in Frankfurt for the red eye leg, overnight to Silicon Valley. Three tickets in the global elite section upstairs in the jumbo jet, where the seats could recline into twin-sized beds. A flight attendant took their suit jackets to hang unwrinkled overnight, and a chef, clad in white hat and apron, prepared dinner in a sizzling, steaming galley kitchen. Leclerc sat near the aisle and Aggarwal, the window. Third row on the left. Guo sat on the right side, in a window seat one and a half staggered rows forward of the two men.

After chicken cordon bleu with roasted summer squash, one flight attendant gathered their ceramic plates and silverware, while a second took their orders for drinks. Her drone soon buzzed into their row. The claws under its belly held a cappuccino for Leclerc and a snifter of cognac for Aggarwal. Reddish-brown, aromatic liquid cradled in one hand, Aggarwal pointed with his other to Leclerc's front, back, and right.

Leclerc read the gesture immediately. He worked the controls in the seat arm for the privacy screens. With a clank and a hum, long and narrow hatches opened in the ceiling, and sound-baffling blackout curtains woven with electronic countermeasure circuits descended.

Aggarwal did the same. His privacy screens were halfway down by the time Leclerc's reached the floor. Electromagnetic strips turned on. Narrow rigid rods snicked together to seal the curtain edges.

Weights held down the hems, secure against stray feet or the wheels of service carts in the aisle.

Could someone still slide a listening device along the floor?

The mechanical hums stopped. The curtains around their seats muffled the sound of the fuel cell turbines on the wings. The only light came from the reading lamps above their heads. Aggarwal's face looked like a craggy mask of shadows.

"You wish to talk?" Leclerc asked.

"No," Aggarwal said around a yawn. "Just want darkness and silence to get some sleep." Aggarwal gestured, belying the words. He pointed to his eyes, his mouth, and then softly tapped his chest where his wearable computer hung inside his shirt.

Leclerc opened up a private communication line. Lowest transmission power, barely detectable outside the curtain even if the ECM circuits magically disappeared.

The muscles around Leclerc's throat and mouth moved as if he spoke with his mouth closed. The patches on the sides of his neck converted the muscle activity into a passable simulation of his voice. "What's going on? Is there something at Lawrence Livermore you haven't told me about?"

Aggarwal replied the same way. The bureaucrat's lips didn't move. Leclerc's wearable staged Aggarwal's voice in his earbuds as if it came from the man's mouth. "I don't know why the laser cannons aren't ready, if that's what you're asking."

"Then what?"

"I've been thinking, you know? About what a pain it's been to work with Orlovsky. And Guo. And stuff that came up back at, you know, Cheltenford Hall."

English was bad enough to have to listen to, but this atrocious American slang.... "What sort of *stuff*?"

"That stuff from Osorio. The gray guy," Aggarwal explained. "That to hostile aliens, we're all going to be the same. Humanist or Traditionalist won't matter, you know?"

"I do."

Aggarwal waggled his finger, like a goalkeeper taunting the opposing striker for missing a penalty. "The differences between us and them won't matter unless we make them matter. Get me?"

Leclerc's skin turned clammy over his throat. The bureaucrat couldn't seriously.... "I don't believe I do."

"The aliens can, like, understand English. They've picked up two centuries of pop radio and old fashioned television. You know, broadcast from Earth. And whatever they got from *Concordia* and its personnel."

"Possibly," Leclerc managed to say.

"If they can't...." Aggarwal shrugged the shoulders of his tailored shirt of blue silk. "Then we're all targets anyway, you know? But if they can...." His eyebrows lowered, like an impatient tutor regarding a slow student. "Then we negotiate with them."

The engines droned. Dark Arctic waters lay eleven kilometers below. "Spare us." Leclerc murmured. "Target the Traditionalists."

"Hell yeah." A brief grin, chased by a brooding look. "Like, why not?"

Leclerc picked his words. "Even if we can talk with them, a negotiation implies we can offer something in return."

Aggarwal waved his hand. Shadows sliding up and down the sides of his fingers made them look like claws unsheathing. "No prob."

Hazy memories of history classes about the loot Napoleon stole from the rest of Europe and the Near East came to Leclerc. "We have no goods they could want. Our artworks would look to them like a madman's look to us." Osorio's other reason why men explored mashed together with the motives behind Napoleon's second marriage. "No rival royal princess to demand as a mate to mother a legitimate dynasty."

"That's not what they want from Earth."

"What do they want?"

"The galaxy for themselves. No other pesky rival spreading across interstellar space. Remember that old Chinese sci-fi book the occupation authorities made our parents read in school? You know, the one where Earth realizes its radio broadcasts are drawing hostile aliens, and all the smart aliens long ago learned to shut up?"

Leclerc gave a blank look. He didn't bother trying to look it up through his wearable.

"Maybe the Chinese occupied France differently than they occupied the U.S. of A." Aggarwal spoke as if he didn't believe it was possible.

"I remember a bonfire in the public square," Leclerc said. "I would have been four years of age. Hundreds of Chinese books and reproduced artworks fed to the flames." Behind a cracked glass, fire consumed a photo of Premier Wáng's bland face. "My parents looked pleased to let out their primal spirits of revenge."

Aggarwal squinted at Leclerc. "You French act all civilized, but you've got a mean streak you let out sometimes."

Leclerc reached for his cappuccino on the tray table cantilevered from the outer armrest. The milk and espresso had cooled to a sludge. Still better than a coffee drink from the break room at mission control. "I don't know the book you refer to, but I take your point. How did Memford put it at Cheltenford? 'The galaxy isn't big enough for the two of us'?"

"He's a joking mofo, but, like, what can you do? But you know what I'm saying."

"We promise the aliens we will cease interstellar exploration if they target Traditionalist sites only." Leclerc gulped the dregs of his cappuccino. He returned it to the tray, cup clinking saucer. "Why would they believe us?"

"Couple reasons. After they wreck the Trads for us, we'll be too busy reorganizing Trad territories in line with proper Humanist principles. And we can't go interstellar without being seen. If we've got enough scopes to see *Concordia* or the bogey across four light-years the aliens must too. They'll see us leaving and send a punitive expedition."

Heartburn crawled up Leclerc's chest. He inclined his head toward Guo. "Won't her people promise the aliens the same?"

A sniff of cognac vapors. "We have the advantage, you know. The Trads are Earth-centric. They think God created the universe, then after thirteen billion years picked out a few prophets of one species on one planet to be best buds with. Getting shown up by aliens with hella higher tech blows that nonsense up."

Leclerc scrunched up his mouth. The Traditionalist mind was more supple than Humanist propaganda would admit.

The bureaucrat's bushy eyebrows danced. "But us? We see the world as it is, and humankind's place in it the same way." The slang dropped out of his voice when he quoted rhetoric from London or Silicon Valley. "We can accept being confined to Sol system, but the Trads can't."

"The aliens won't know that—"

"Until we tell them. Just like we have to give them the coordinates of targets. Not just official Trad facilities, but the hideouts where their leadership would, like, take shelter. We'll need to get that from intel."

"Your plan has not been approved from higher channels." Leclerc's voice sounded like threads worn bare.

"Not yet," Aggarwal said around a sip of cognac. "But don't worry, it's going to be. I need you to work out which transmitter we should use to max the odds the aliens hear us without, you know, her overhearing." His eyes flicked in Guo's direction.

"And if higher channels reject your plan?"

"They won't. I got to tell them soon as we land, because they might think it up themselves, you know?"

"But they could decide your plan carries too much risk." Leclerc's hand groped the air for more words. "The aliens could decide any faction negotiating for their help against other humans is so manipulative it will eventually turn against them."

"Turn against them with what? We'd be like soldiers with guns trying to take out the cannon of a tank."

"We don't know the aliens's minds," Leclerc said. "Let alone how to read them."

Aggarwal mulled over this cognac, then shooed the objection away with his free hand. "Either way, we get smashed flat. Same risk. What gives the bigger reward? We gotta play the odds. Which is offer the aliens this deal. Even if, like, *higher channels—*" Aggarwal larded the phrase with sarcasm. "—tell me no."

"You would defy them?"

A quick shake of the head. "Better to ask forgiveness than permission, you know? And you'll set us up so the bigwigs won't know we sent the message, same as Guo won't."

Leclerc swallowed down a dry throat. "I fear too much ill would come to us. From London, St. Petersburg, or the aliens. Or all three."

"How are the Trads going to know?" The shadows cast by the reading lamps turned Aggarwal's eyes into deep pits. "Unless you tell them."

"I would do no such thing." Did sweat trickle down his bald scalp? God willing, no.

"Good. Because it would be a damn shame if you got reassigned to Diego Garcia. Or if something bad happened to your wife and daughter."

Sweat bloomed then. The climate control in the global elite cabin whisked it away, chilling Leclerc's head. He groped for the armrest and clutched it. His fingers turned white against the padded plastic. At least the armrest was real and would not change out from under him.

Aggarwal reached into the underseat storage. Zips and hook-and-loop fabric scritches meant he dug into his roller carryon bag. A moment later, he leaned against his seat back with a black padded sleepmask between his thick fingers. "So work out where we should send the message from. I need it by the time we land."

He pressed a button on the armrest. By the time his seat reclined to full horizontal, Aggarwal had the sleep mask over his eyes.

Leclerc sat in the dim light. His heart eased its thumping.

Nervous energy bled from his limbs, turning his arms limp. The last of his cold sweat dried.

Aggarwal snored.

Damn you.

Leclerc cycled slow breaths. What could he do?

Go to Guo? Simple. Demagnetize the curtain halves, slip through, and do the same across the aisle a row and a half ahead.

And then? Become an intel asset for the Traditionalists, to be sacrificed if her faction deemed it their best play?

What if the Traditionalists plotted the same treachery?

And though he couldn't see them, cameras and microphones covered Guo every moment since they'd changed planes in Frankfurt. The miniaturized and high-tech equivalent of the young Russians aiding them around the shipyard. If he went to her, he couldn't escape the surveillance.

Exile to a flyspeck island would be heaven compared to the fate Aggarwal would inflict on him.

Go over Aggarwal's head? How did the Americans put it? Blow the whistle. One of the figures at Cheltenford Hall might take his side.

How many would take Aggarwal's?

Leclerc dabbed his forehead with his fingers. His stomach turned sour. He had no choice. Find a transmitter on which the Traditionalists could not eavesdrop....

Unless he *accidentally* picked the wrong one. *I had no idea they had a listening post ten kilometers away.*

A pleased feeling sloshed through him, like waves.

Breaking on rocks.

If the Traditionalists learned the Humanists plotted against them, they would pull out of the joint defense project. Humanist lasers mounted on tank chassis, or even airplanes, would lack the power of a submarine's nuclear reactor and would be naked to the sky. Traditionalist submarines with second-tier directed energy weapons would ping off a spaceship hull hardened against years of relativistic travel. Work together, or get divided and conquered.

Or obliterated.

Give Aggarwal a site. That did not mean the Humanist leaders would approve his plan. And despite his bluster, Aggarwal would not go behind their backs if they rejected it.

A trickle of hope ran through Leclerc.

Next to him, Aggarwal snored, mouth slack, drool at its corner.

CHAPTER 12

25 JULY 2132

Sunlight streamed into the conference room through the windows from the courtyard. Outside, a gnarled tree's branches twined over benches made of thick planks. A rustic style, from a quarter of a millennium ago, before freeways and tract houses smothered chaparral hills and redwood forests.

Inside, the odor of over-roasted coffee in biodegradable foam cups. The squeak and rustle of black mesh roller chairs. Plain off-white walls dressed up with whimsical artworks. Pride of place went to a broad canvas of Native Americans in feathered headdresses standing in front of an antique bomber with propellers on the wings. *Planes Indians.*

The California way. Decorate a soulless, mass-produced building with a few absurd touches, and the peasants will be content in their cubicle farm while the elites profit off their labors.

No peasants lingered in the conference room now. Leclerc,

Aggarwal, and Guo sat in the middle of one of the table's long sides, facing the windows. On the other side, backlit by cloudless pale blue sky, Lawrence Livermore's higher managers scowled and crossed their arms.

"If only you'd told us," said de la Cruz, the laboratory's CEO. A man about Leclerc's age, with shrewd brown eyes and a beard so uniformly brown it had to be dyed. His gaze darted between the three of them before settling on Aggarwal. "Aliens coming to Earth with unknown intent? I would have put every spare man-hour on the laser project."

Aggarwal raised his hand. "I would have told you if I could. London put me on, you know, a short leash. Need to know. Didn't want to cause a panic if the aliens drove full speed into the sun."

Shrewd eyes regarded Guo. "And your people?"

Her businesslike expression matched her gray skirt-suit and the slender silver watch limp around her wrist. "It is not our place to question your internal procedures." Her tone implied the Trads should have done so anyway, but so subtly Aggarwal gave no sign of hearing a rebuke in her words.

De la Cruz, on the other hand.... He kept his arms folded over his chest as he spoke to Aggarwal. "I get the need for security. I answer to London, too. But you can't downplay the priority with one hand, then bitch us out with the other for putting the project low on the stack."

Aggarwal's thick eyebrows bunched. Then his chin dipped to the side, dragging his gaze to a blank spot on the tabletop. His wearable sent information to his eyes only.

He drew a long breath and returned his eyes to de la Cruz. A minor interruption? "Am I, like, complaining?"

Behind his far shoulder, Guo raised one eyebrow a couple of millimeters. Leclerc mirrored her expression. Of course he'd complained, from the moment the three of them had arrived at the former American national laboratory, and even after the reason for the delay—his own secrecy—had become clear.

"It's water under the bridge. Just put it on the top of your stack. Now."

De la Cruz and his subordinates grunted and shifted their weight. Shared glances plainly showed they sent private messages among themselves. "We can't argue the urgency," de la Cruz said. "Though we'll get more productivity from our people if they understand the stakes. How far down the hierarchy can we share the news?"

"Anyone with the standard security clearance is authorized to know aliens are coming."

De la Cruz pivoted his gaze to Leclerc. "How long till their ship will be visible?"

"University astronomy departments in the southern hemisphere will pick it up within a month. Two billion people will see it with the naked eye by late November or early December."

Brown eyes met his. "Got it."

Leclerc's cheeks flexed in a faint smile. A good leader knew when to enforce the rules and when to break them. De la Cruz would overlook his people leaking the news to their friends and loved ones when the alien ship grew closer.

Forget a tropical beach in August. Provincial towns in the middle of continents would see an inflow of tourists come December. Turning into a flood, as rumors spread and people panicked.

Would the aliens strike *Concordia* mission control? If they did, would their weapons wreak collateral damage as far as the farmhouse where his wife and daughter slept?

Leclerc reached for his coffee cup, pulled his hand back, made an impotent fist. He did all he could for them, now.

Aggarwal leaned forward. "How much longer? To get the first set to Russia?"

"We'll get the first one out in two days," said de la Cruz. "The next three two days after. You have the transport planes ready?"

"Waiting at the air force base." Aggarwal waved his hand toward the north.

De la Cruz rolled back his chair and stood. "My team has a lot to do. We'll get started. The three of you—" He glanced at Guo. "—are welcome to use the conference room—"

"Nah, we'll head back to the hotel." Aggarwal's tone sounded too casual.

The meeting broke up. De la Cruz and Aggarwal shook hands across the table. The groups melded at the door. Guo raised her hand to waist height, ready to shake, but no one offered to do so. Did California Humanists still resent all Chinese people for the excesses of the Wáng regime's occupation half a century ago? If so, Guo showed no sign of offense.

Another explanation for why no one shook her hand came at their hotel. If the tower of concrete and glass, next to the freeway and surrounded by a parking lot of baking hot asphalt, merited the title. *Hôtel George V* it was not. In the lobby, while air conditioning unglued their sweaty shirts from their backs, a ping announced the arrival of an elevator.

Aggarwal gestured for Guo to enter. "We'll take the next one."

"Till the morning," she said. She extended her hand.

Leclerc reached for it—

Thick hands landed on his shoulders and pushed him away from Guo's outstretched hand. "Actually, we need to, you know, talk to the front desk. Later," Aggarwal added over his shoulder to her.

Guo lowered her hand as if she expected the snub. "Good evening." She entered the elevator while Aggarwal hustled Leclerc toward the front desk.

Slanted parallelograms of afternoon sunlight glowed on the synthetic marble floor. Aggarwal guided Leclerc to an unused sitting area, stood him with legs against a low brown table covered with tourist brochures. Aggarwal spoke in a harsh whisper. "Kee-rist, are you, like, stupid?"

"Apparently."

"She was trying to plant a bug on you, you know?"

Leclerc raised an eyebrow. "I've shaken her hand a dozen times and screened myself after each. She's never planted a listening device on me before."

"She's sly. She suspects what you and I talked about on the plane." Aggarwal lowered his voice. "I called London earlier today. They want to talk about my proposal."

"They messaged you when we talked with de la Cruz."

"Like, what, it was that obvious? You see, that's why she's suspicious."

Leclerc shrugged. "One must be careful, no matter what kind of threat faces all of us. Shall we order room service and prepare for the call?"

"Nah. They want to talk now. It's middle of the night there, you know?" Aggarwal grinned. "They're going to say yes."

Leclerc's fingertips dabbed his mustache. He couldn't look Aggarwal in the eye. "We won't know until we talk."

"Then come the hell up and talk to them."

Aggarwal had pulled enough rank to land a corner suite on the top floor. Broad views of tract housing, shimmering in the heat of late summer, stretched to rocky hills splotched with green. From near the balcony doors in the living room, the rustle of traffic on the freeway barely made it through the double panes of insulated glass. Aggarwal had laid out security scanners and active ECM devices and their flattened domes, roughly the size and shape of a man's thumbnail, dotted the balcony railing. Their chameleon paint made them almost invisible. The past few months of travel had trained Leclerc's eye to them.

He rested his hand on the handle of the sliding balcony door. Tension bled out of his shoulders. The world was ruled by men—and, these centuries, women also—steeped in secrets and lies. Such is how human history had been for ten thousand years. Only an American, one of the legion creeping along the freeway below to their quarter-acre lots, would believe their Constitution was a magic spell by which the world could be governed openly, for the good of all.

But if it could....

"Don't open the door," Aggarwal said.

Leclerc drew back his hand. He put on a face to show he hadn't planned to. "It's far too hot outside."

"And don't pull the curtain either. How small a drone can Guo fly? How well can it read lips?"

Leclerc nodded. He pushed down a virtual slider provided through his wearable from the room's computer. The curtains, rotated a quarter turn compared to the ones on the flight from Frankfurt, narrowed the rectangle of bright square until they completely snuffed it out. The lamps around the room looked pallid in comparison, like wizened and senile stars.

"Sit," Aggarwal said. He plopped onto the couch, gently enough not to spill his glass of Scotch from the wet bar in the corner. Like all the furniture, the couch was an attempt at minimalism that simply looked cheap. At least the cushions were spongy under Leclerc's rear.

"Talk only if they ask you a question, you know? Like, I mean it. You better the hell be on board with me."

"Where else would I be?" He regretted the words an instant later. Would Aggarwal take the words as a hint he plotted defection to Guo and the Traditionalists?

"A hardship station without your family. Permanently." Aggarwal gulped Scotch. "Here we go."

Both their wearables made connections. They needed a few seconds to complete authentication up and down the satellite link to London. Enough time for Leclerc to wish he'd gotten a glass of wine before they started.

Two figures manifested in the room. Leclerc's wearable projected them onto virtual chairs in front of the television and chest of drawers on the far wall. The software even gave them virtual shadows cast by the room's lamps.

Two figures. Rubik with the beehive hairdo. Makeup as deft at midnight as it would have been that morning. The sarcastic American, who today wore a different faux-antique rock band T-shirt, this one festooned with a leering tongue jutting between thick lips.

Leclerc shifted his weight, trying to get comfortable. Where were the others?

"Good evening," Aggarwal said. "Thank you for getting back to me so quickly."

"You got our attention," said Memford. "Side with the aliens against the real enemy? Something out of an UltraHistory game."

Aggarwal's gaze darted around Memford's face. "I never played it. But maybe Leclerc—"

Leclerc shook his head. "I know it was popular with *Concordia* personnel on the journey out, but I have never had time for it."

"Your loss." Memford slid his gaze back to Aggarwal. "Here's what happened so far. We met with Osorio over dinner about how to take your plan to Neville. He said no."

Aggarwal sagged over his gut. "Oh." He gulped down some of his Scotch.

Leclerc's head eased back against the wall. Finally, something solid instead of Aggarwal's scheming. They would focus on the alien threat to all humankind instead of the petty rivalry with the Traditionalists.

Rubik spoke. Months in Russia had better tuned his ear for her Eastern European accent. "But we understand it might be possible to send a message without him noticing? Is this true? Mr. Leclerc?"

His head jerked forward. He swallowed around a lump in his throat. Lie to them.

And face the music when someone else told them the truth? "We can transmit directionally toward the alien ship from an isolated station. Diego Garcia, say. Neither the Traditionalists nor anyone else would be likely to pick up the transmission. But such a transmission might leave records, logs... station personnel might talk—"

"We can minimize those risks," she said. Her soft blue eyes met his gaze.

She couldn't talk of murdering everyone posted on Diego Garcia. Could she?

"So we *can* make the offer to the aliens," said Memford.

Rubik sharpened her gaze. "The only question is, should we?"

Aggarwal spoke with such animation ice cubes tinkled in his glass. "There's so much to gain and nothing more to lose. If the aliens ignore our message or say no, they were going to bomb us anyway, right?"

"How would they tell us *no?*" she asked. "Mr. Leclerc?"

The way his stomach clenched, wine would have been a bad choice. "They would transmit to Earth, I should think."

"Yes, obviously. Could the Traditionalists pick up an alien transmission?"

Leclerc let out a breath. "Almost certainly."

"Which would alert the Traditionalists to our double-dealing. We should not risk that."

Memford turned to her, putting the sharp lines of his nose and brow into profile. "When we transmit to them, we give them a code to use if they reply."

"The Traditionalists would pick up the alien transmission regardless whether the message content were in the clear or coded." Rubik raised an eyebrow at Leclerc.

"That's true," Leclerc said.

Memford gave him a passing glance, then aimed his gaze at Rubik. "Or we tell the aliens not to reply."

"Would they heed that?" she said.

Aggarwal piped up. "Why wouldn't they? We're willing to work with them, you know. It's such a good offer. We'll stay in Sol system forever, give them the rest of the galaxy. If I were them, like, I'd take it."

Memford nodded.

Rubik tapped her cheek with one slender finger. "Possibly. But you assume their minds work like ours. What do we know of them? They journeyed to Alpha Centauri a million years ago and lay dormant, or their robots lay dormant, until *Concordia*'s people roused them. Have we learned anything more?"

Aggarwal turned his scowling eyebrows on Leclerc. Answer the question put to you and nothing more.

"*Non*," said Leclerc. Good God, man, you're so nervous you're slipping into French. "No."

"Meaning they could respond to our message in a way we wouldn't expect. Perhaps even switch to the suicide mission we feared they might be launching."

Memford rolled his eyes. His next words came from the aliens's point of view. "We were going to bomb them into the Stone Age, but they won't work together, so let's destroy their planet. And kill ourselves in the process."

"They're aliens," Rubik said.

"They might think differently, but they aren't going to commit suicide."

Aggarwal cleared his throat. "Something else to think about. What if the Trads offer the aliens the same deal? All the more reason we should transmit."

Leclerc opened his mouth. Yesterday the Traditionalists were too human-centric to accept junior status in the galaxy. But now...

He mashed his lips together. Yesterday Aggarwal had threatened his family.

Rubik pivoted her gaze to Leclerc. "Can we detect if they do?"

"I assume we gather signals intelligence from near Traditionalist ground stations. If so, we can."

"Unless it's as isolated as Diego Garcia—"

Memford snorted. "There's no place occupied by the Trads as isolated as Diego Garcia—"

"Could they put a transmission array on a ship? Or a submarine? Mr. Leclerc?"

He worked his mouth before words came out. "I expect it is possible."

"Making it more logical for us to transmit. If it's possible, the Trads will do it, you know."

The blonde looked thoughtful. "There's another factor. *Concordia* and the ground stations on Four Freedoms."

"What factor?" Memford asked. "The aliens killed them all. A damn shame but it's water under the bridge. We have to do what's best for us now."

"Did the aliens kill them?"

Memford bugged his eyes at her. "*Concordia* hasn't sent anything since January." He aimed his hatchet face at Leclerc.

Leclerc felt sweat on his bare scalp. "That's true."

Back to Rubik. Memford idly rubbed the rock band logo with his knuckles. "What the hell else do you think could've happened?"

"*Concordia* stopped transmitting two days before the alien ship launched from the surface," she said. "Yes?"

Leclerc nodded. With luck, they would ask him no more—

She turned to him. "Have you seen any sign of destruction of *Concordia*?"

Aggarwal and Memford scowled at him. He chose words like steps through a minefield. "No. The ship is still in orbit. We conclude this because its life support system still glows in the infrared at room temperature."

"The ground stations on the planet?"

"Not bombarded. At least not with the power the alien ship is capable of."

"Not even the one near the alien facility?"

"If it survived the alien ship's launch, then it should be intact."

Memford stretched his hands over his head. The jutting tongue on his T-shirt slid up his chest. To Rubik, he asked, "So what?"

"Over a hundred human beings are their hostages."

"Which means the aliens aren't genocidal," Memford said. "They can be reasoned with. We can send them a message."

She sagged back in her chair. "You see no common cause with the Trads? Our shared humanity, our joint mission to the nearest star, mean less than the chance to defeat them? You have played UltraHistory. What are the lessons from it?"

"The bitterest rivals are those in the same niche." Memford emphasized the last word. And mispronounced it *nitch*. Leclerc's teeth ground together.

"Isn't there another lesson?" Rubik asked. "Inviting a more powerful outsider to help you against your rivals ends up giving the outsider dominance over you both. That was a recurring theme in Western European colonialism and imperialism. Play one faction of natives against the other."

The American scowled at her. "If the outsider's going to dominate you anyway, better to be the beta dog than the bitch."

"You are ever the fountain of colorful metaphors," the blonde said. Her beehive hairdo quivered as she turned to Leclerc. "The intent behind the submarines and laser cannons is to fight against domination. Can we defeat the aliens?"

He dabbed his fingers at his mustache, then pulled them away. "The submersible laser platforms we're building with the Traditionalists give us the best chance of success."

"'Best chance?'" Memford asked. "Give us a number. One percent? 99%?"

Leclerc's voice sounded small in his own ears. "We know too little about the alien ship to say."

"Any chance is worth the attempt," said Rubik. Her gaze hardened at Memford. "You would be the capo in the gulag, forever. If we fight and lose, we would be the prisoner forever instead. Either way we remain in the prison camp. But if we fight and win... Mr. Leclerc, what could we do with the aliens's technology?"

"I should think it obvious. Defend Sol system if they launch another expedition against us. And someday, explore and settle the galaxy for ourselves."

Aggarwal stole a glance at Memford, then chimed in. "Explore and settle it with the Trads."

Leclerc mashed his lips together. He wanted to push back, against Aggarwal's scowl, against Memford's willingness to be the aliens's beaten dog. Images of his wife and daughter, and a muscle squad sent by Aggarwal, held his tongue.

Rubik spoke instead, to Memford, as if Aggarwal was of no consequence. "You'd rather rule in hell than share half of heaven?"

Memford sat back. His fingertips drummed his chest through his T-shirt. "I'd go all in on fighting the aliens, if I knew I had pocket aces in the hole. But if I've only got 2-8 off suit, forget it. Better to save my chips for a better hand."

"Poker metaphors, I take it? But I do follow your logic," she said. "Mr. Leclerc, how much more can you tell us about the alien ship?"

Leclerc waggled his hands. "I've told you all I know as of now."

"Then learn more and tell us again. Soon." Rubik turned to Memford. "How much time will you give him?"

"You said college telescopes will be able to see the alien ship in a few more weeks?"

Mouth too dry to speak, Leclerc nodded.

"September 1," Memford said. "We meet then. Just the four of us. And nobody says a damn word to Osorio, Neville, anybody." Sharp eyes met Leclerc's gaze.

"Very well," he said. Not a victory, but a reprieve. He let out a breath as the others dropped out of the call.

Aggarwal's bushy eyebrows narrowed and lowered, then eased. "You know, he's right. I only wanted to play the aliens against the Trads if, like, we couldn't beat the aliens and, you know, steal their energy tech."

"Yes. Clearly." Leclerc's pulse knocked in his neck. Aggarwal, vain and self-absorbed, as usual. Holding his fate, his family's fate, in veiny hands.

"Damn, I'm hungry. I'll order us room service. Steaks? Grown in a vat, but it's California."

Stomach still flopping, Leclerc said, "Something lighter, for me."

"Nah, two steaks. Filet Mignon. That's French, right?" Aggarwal swiped the air. His finger made a final jab. "On its way."

The robotic cart arrived twenty minutes later. Two hunks of

synthetic bovine muscle, identical in size and shape, and equally bloody red when sliced into. Baked potatoes the size of American footballs, smothered in butter and cheese and sour cream. At least Aggarwal let him beg off from alcohol and drink a bottle of sparkling water instead.

As they ate, Aggarwal went on at length about how they would play the angles, regardless whether the next meeting resulted in collaboration with the Traditionalists or treachery against them. High ranking positions in a Humanist interstellar colonization agency or a bureau manning the phones, listening for orders for Humanist-controlled Earth to come from their superiors at Alpha Centauri.

"Or wherever they're really from. I guess we'll find out if we steal their tech and carry the war to them. Damn, we're going places. And I need you, you know? You've got science chops. My right-hand man. How do you say that in French?"

"I don't know the term," Leclerc said. Despite the adrenaline hangover from the meeting upsetting his stomach, he ate even faster, in a bid to get out of Aggarwal's suite as soon as he could.

But when Leclerc returned to his room, two floors down and near the clanking machinery of the elevator shaft, he couldn't relax. Opening the blinds to the evening, where headlights and advertising signs washed out the stars into grayness, put him back on edge. Closing them left him in the dark with pangs for Sybil. One lamp emphasized the gloom outside its reach. All the lamps filled the room with sterile whiteness.

Finally, he gave up and went downstairs to the bar. His stomach could handle a glass of wine, now. It might soothe his nerves for the night.

In the bar, hanging lamps formed tiny pockets of light over scattered tables. Water trickled down a slab fountain of slate mounted on the back wall. A popular song from the '8os, cheerful with hope for the liberated world, whispered from hidden speakers. Few customers. Three businessmen hulked over a round table, voices bragging about reaming and shafting a competitor, glances flicking over to the only woman in the room.

Guo. She wore the same gray skirt-suit as earlier. No traditional Chinese dress here, deep in Humanist country. Gaze engrossed by a private virtual. On her black veneered table, a goblet held a pink drink garnished with orange and pineapple wedges slipped onto the rim. The tropical beach he'd wanted with Sybil suddenly receded another million miles.

Maybe her people knew more about the alien ship. Enough to answer the question Memford had posed to him.

Or maybe her people plotted the same betrayal as Aggarwal.

Only one way to find out.

Leclerc went to her. He'd almost reached her tall table before she looked up. She raised her hand from the goblet. Her slack watch slid down her wrist. Silver glinted in the pocket of light before her watch fell below the cuff of her jacket.

"Care for company?" he asked.

"You wish to be seen with me?" She spoke with a smile, her accent noticeable. A twitch of her fingers reminded him of the cloud of minuscule Humanist counterintel drones that had to surround her.

"We have a common cause, do we not?"

She nodded and beckoned at a stool, a tall and wiry thing of alloy tubes and strappy plastic. He pulled it out and sat a third of the way around the table from her. His feet dangled off the floor like a child's. He faced a glass wall looking out at a swimming pool, deep blue and quiet at this hour. The three businessmen loomed in the corner of his eye.

They gave him and Guo some harsh looks. When they pushed their elbows off their table, Leclerc clenched his fist, below the tabletop on the side away from them. His feet searched behind his heels for a crosspiece between the chair legs, a base to spring from into action. Childhood brawls and martial arts classes. He'd never won, but every time he'd drawn blood.

Last boasts, about screwing and sodomizing their competitor, then the businessmen left.

He let out a breath.

Guo glanced at his fist. "You were concerned about them?"

"One should be prepared." He opened his hand, shook out his fingers. "Just as we are attempting to prepare for…" It wouldn't do to talk in public about invading aliens. He groped for euphemisms until the example of the businessmen prodded some loose. "New entrants in our industry."

She smiled at that. No teeth showed, but the expression wrinkled her eyes. She gave a little nod into the space she'd stared at when he came in. "I was attempting to do just that."

The machinery behind the bar gurgled. A hum of motors above him came closer. A robotic arm extended from the ceiling track and rested a glass of red wine on the table.

Leclerc's heart thumped. "Do you have some business intelligence I don't?" He sipped his wine. And winced. Too sweet, too cold.

"No. Only the same reports from the same field offices as you."

No surprise. The Traditionalists couldn't set up a parallel array of telescopes and radio receivers across Sol system without Humanist intel noticing. Assuming his side's intel service would bother telling him.

Guo lifted the goblet. She brought the straw to her mouth effortlessly, gaze on him the while. "I was reviewing the data we had, to see if we could better understand the capabilities and strategy of our competitors."

He wished she meant Aggarwal, Memford, and their counterparts in the Traditionalist hierarchy. But what she talked about touched on the facts he needed to gather over the next month about the real threat to all. He leaned forward. "What did you conclude?"

"Nothing, yet. But one thing I've been puzzling over. They had a steady business model for many quarters. Why did they change it now?"

Leclerc sipped the bad wine. The saccharine taste shocked him to alertness. "They decided we could be outcompeted."

"*They*? Did the push come from the bottom, from their regional office? Or from the CEO far off at corporate headquarters?"

"The regional office. After all, so large an organization cannot make decisions so quickly."

Guo's hand curled around the goblet stem without touching it. "Which brings up something else. An organization so large and founded so long ago should be active in other territories, shouldn't it?"

The metaphors broke down. The aliens arrived at Alpha Centauri a million years ago, give or take. Even if computers back-tracked the galactic orbits of all likely stars within a hundred light-years of Sol, Leclerc could not with confidence point to the star they'd journeyed from.

But he didn't have to. The vast power wielded by the aliens allowed them to travel at relativistic speeds. That same power could easily fuel exponential growth in their population and the number of machines serving them. In a million years, the aliens or their robots should have explored every system in the galaxy.

The aliens should have come to Earth when humankind's ancestors bore weapons no more advanced than spears.

His wearable sent him a chime, and the jangling icon of a ringing antique telephone. The faint smile on Guo's face told him she called even before he read her name under the icon.

He opened the connection. One icon showed the call was encrypted. He assumed Humanist counterintel recorded it as well, through some backdoor hard coded into his wearable's CPU.

Guo's voice came to him as if from her closed mouth. "I lack proof, but I strongly suspect the aliens are extinct everywhere except Bravo Charlie."

"Plausible."

"If so, I further suspect the Alpha Centauri expedition was the first they ever launched, and the extinction event happened while the alien ship was underway, or shortly after its arrival there."

Leclerc sipped the bad wine before replying. "You think this because...?"

"An extinction event could devastate one system, but not multiple systems at once."

"Not instantly, no. But a massive gamma ray burst propagating at light speed is close enough to instantaneous after a million years."

"True," Guo said. Her solemn tone clashed with the bright yellow and orange fruit garnishing her drink. "But an extinction event to devastate multiple systems could only have happened early in the aliens' expansion. Later, they would have spread too far to be destroyed by any single event."

Leclerc reached for his wine glass, stopped short. "I'm following."

"Consider. If the aliens occupied other systems than their home-world's and Alpha Centauri, and their homeworld suffered the extinction event, their other outposts would have survived. And with the energy at their disposal, those outposts could undertake exponential growth and soon enough launch galactic exploration vessels traveling at relativistic speeds."

"Getting us back to where we were. And because that is not the galaxy we see..." Leclerc's smile pierced the gloom that brought him here. "The one alien ship is the only thing between us and galactic colonization."

The smile shrank a little. That damned American. Wanting to be the capo, controlling all the other prisoners inside the barbed wire, when the prison camp's main gate was wide open and only a single guard could stop them.

Would that fact be enough to persuade him to fight with the Traditionalists, instead of against them?

Another thought tugged Leclerc's gaze to the black veneer. He pondered. "Why didn't the aliens at Alpha Centauri follow the same path of exponential growth and exploration?"

"That I do not know," Guo said. "Does any answer occur to you?"

In their pocket of light, he alone with this woman he could not fully trust, with silly drinks on the table and half-remembered songs over the sound system, the question seemed unreal. Extinction event or not, assuming exponential growth, the aliens should have reached Earth hundreds of thousands of years ago. And dominated it.

Or destroyed it.

"Perhaps we should not assume exponential growth."

Guo's forehead creased. "Any known biological population—"

"Which this is not."

"Known? Or biological?"

"Let's start with known."

Guo gave her head a little shake, enough to send a ripple through the in-curling ends of her glossy black hair. "It seems unlikely that biology would follow different laws on different planets. Give a species enough food and habitat, and its population will grow. Even at a rate that would seem slow if lived through, a doubling time of a century, their population would grow by a factor of one million in just two thousand years."

And one trillion in four thousand years.... an eyeblink in the vast gulf of time between the aliens' arrival at Alpha Centauri and now.

"And if the ship's crew and passengers are not biological?" Guo asked. "Robots left behind by extinct masters, or the masters were robots to begin with? Given the energy available to them, they could manufacture more of themselves with population doubling times of days, not years."

Leclerc squirmed on his high seat, sifting over her words. "You assume the alien survivors at Alpha Centauri kept the technical know-how to power exponential growth."

Another forehead crease. "The exhaust of their ship shows they wield great power."

"It shows they have a power plant. It doesn't prove they built the power plant at Alpha Centauri."

"Ah." She gave her drink a brief slow stir with the straw. "I don't think so. Even if the original factories were lost with their homeworld, they had enough time at Alpha Centauri to build new power plants by reverse engineering."

Leclerc mulled over names grooved into his memory over the past decade. "You can't assume that. *Concordia*'s chief propulsion engineer, one of your people—"

"Jaeger."

"—is highly skilled at managing the ship's Bussard ramjet. It doesn't prove he could build one from scratch."

Guo sipped. Her drink fully receded from the tip of the pineapple wedge. "Perhaps. But how else could they have a working power plant after a million years, other than building it recently?"

"With energies so vast at their disposal, they may well have developed materials built to last. Which is a further argument for them not bringing the know-how to build new power plants with them. The ones they had on their ship could have been enough to fly to Alpha Centauri and back to their homeworld."

Guo shook her head, and for a moment he glimpsed the steel that made most workers at mission control nervous around her. "You assume they were explorers, like *Concordia*, and not permanent settlers. You assume the ship coming to Earth is the one they flew to Bravo Charlie."

Leclerc crossed his arms and quirked his mouth at her. "You were the one speaking of the extinction happening at a time early in the aliens's expansion. My assumptions fit with yours."

"Fair enough. But with the power they can use, and the need for self-sufficiency required for any interstellar mission, I expect even explorers would be able to turn into settlers with a population capable of exponential growth." She waved his prior objections away. The links in her wristwatch band tinkled together. "The question remains. Why didn't they?"

Leclerc reached for the bad wine, but couldn't lower himself to take another sip. The red in the glass reminded him of the rust-covered desert in the middle of Bravo Charlie's single continent. A continent teeming with native life in its myriad forms.

A continent with no sign intelligent life had ever trod it, let alone had a million years to build on it a high-tech civilization.

"They died out." Possibilities came to him. "A disease, perhaps, or a micronutrient deficiency. Or a suicidal madness in the wake of their homeworld's destruction."

"Possible. If they were biological."

Leclerc said, "If that ship is robotic, they programmed the robots for a cause other than filling the galaxy with copies of themselves."

"To wait for visitors, then attack? A poor strategy, for multiple reasons." Guo ticked the first one off on her fingers. "At the theater-of-operations level of strategy, they run the risk that the visitors arrive at Bravo Charlie near the end of their expansion through the galaxy. Their one robotic ship would attack a foe already lodged in a hundred billion systems and defended with technology a million years more advanced then their own."

"Unless they are monitoring the skies for signs of advanced civilizations. Perhaps they would launch many more ships, perhaps even before the advanced civilizations came to visit, if they saw evidence of them."

"If so, we have more evidence for the rarity of intelligent life." Guo turned thoughtful eyes to her tropical goblet.

Leclerc bobbed his head. "The second reason?" As the words came out, his head froze and his eyes went wide. Another puzzle. He held the new question in his thoughts and half-listened to her next words.

"At the grand strategic level, if they wanted their robots to eventually expand through the galaxy, they would not wait." Her eyebrows nudged upward. "Something else came to your mind."

"How did the alien robots know to send a ship to Sol system?"

Guo considered. "They extracted intel from *Concordia* or the ground expeditions? They watched the lines of approach from all the nearby stars? Perhaps both?"

A scene from a second-rate movie. A robot with an elongated, insectile head aimed a power drill at a human captive's eyes. Leclerc shuddered, refocused. "Yes, of course. An unimportant question. Back to where we were. The alien robots were not programmed to lurk then attack? Possibly, but that implies the aliens thought as well as you do."

"You flatter me, but I'm not more intelligent than a species that can extract energy from vacuum."

The lights dimmed. A note appeared in the corner of his vision, verifying his room number to charge his glass of wine. A bad value at half the price.

"Hotel bars close so early? Americans." Leclerc rolled his eyes.

"We must leave soon," Guo said.

"I will be quick. Intelligence is not a unitary thing, but a set of modules. The aliens could combine engineering brilliance with strategic ineptitude, or religious motivations running counter to the needs of pure strategy. Perhaps they felt compelled to offer hypothetical aliens—us—a fair fight."

"Or they did not want their robots to expand through the galaxy."

The mount flange of a robotic arm assembly clattered along the ceiling tracks to the back corner.

"Then what did they want?" Leclerc asked over the hum of the assembly's motor. The arms extended to a high chair. Lifted, inverted, set it on the tabletop.

Guo climbed down from her chair. Half her drink remained on the table. "We will not find the answer tonight. But it would be good to find it before their ship arrives."

CHAPTER 13

30 AUGUST 2132 (EARTH REFERENCE FRAME) | 3 NOVEMBER 2128 (*NAPOLEON* REFERENCE FRAME)

THE SHIP BACKED TOWARD EARTH. A little over 3000 AU, merely five hundred billion kilometers, to go. A stone's throw compared to the trillions of klicks they'd already crossed.

They traveled at a third of light speed, but slowed more every second. The stars visible in the fore cameras looked normal. Mathematically, they still had to be red-shifted, but at levels Jaeger's eye could not see. In the center of the fore view, Alpha Centauri, among the brightest in the sky.... and so small against the vast backdrop of stars that it seemed miraculous anyone could have found the Octalien legacy on a single planet orbiting one of its member stars.

The surviving Octaliens had bent all their efforts to saving other intelligent life from their self-destructive fate. The thought humbled Jaeger, even now, over three subjective years since they'd deciphered the Octaliens's message. He would raise a toast to their images lining the walls of the chapel next Atrocious Wine Day.

Six weeks till then.

Three and a half months until arrival at Sol system.

It didn't seem that way. Earth was still invisible through the glow of the drive. Not even Sol's rays could pierce the intense shine. But the mission of the five of them would enter the next phase far too soon, given all the work they still had to do.

"Hit the targets first, broadcast later," McIlroy said. He jabbed his fork into a piece of protein textured and flavored like beef.

The five of them sat around the dining table at one end of the rec room. They'd figured out the controls for the Octaliens's shape-changing alloys and created this room, the third largest in the ship, behind the basketball court and the chapel. Plastic forks and knives scraped over paper plates, and aromas of cracked pepper, fresh-fabbed bread, and a robust red wine filled the air.

"Right," Jaeger said. "When we hit the hydrogen collector at Jupiter, they'll know *Napoleon*'s mission." *Concordia* had fueled up there, to get enough in the tank for the boost phase up to 0.04 *c*, when interstellar hydrogen proved dense enough for the ship's scoop to absorb it. Knocking out the hydrogen collector would prove the 'aliens' wanted to deny the galaxy to the natives of Sol system.

"I reckon I wasn't clear. I meant the targets we'll hit on Earth."

Ulanovas fingered his sandy blond hair back from his eyes. "We strike more fear into them with a message. Fear will drive them to cooperate, okay?"

"A message would give civilians notice to evacuate the target sites," Annike said with a nod.

Seated next to her, Jaeger put down his fork and reached along the table. His fingers, callused from engineering work, slid over the smooth skin on the back of her hand. "Unfortunately, it would give the Humanist and Trad leaderships time to evacuate too."

Her brown eyes turned to him. "Is that a bad thing? We want the factions to unify. If we can do it without killing a single person, shouldn't we?"

Jaeger squeezed her hand. "I hear you, love. But the leaderships might be too fixed in their ways to cooperate, even against hostile aliens attacking them both. It might be better if they died in our operation and more flexible minds took their place."

"Please don't euphemize. It would be a good thing if our attack killed them. I see the logic, even though I don't agree with it."

Marie set down her glass of wine. Her voice had a jaunty tinge of Gallic cynicism. "The inner parties will survive."

At her side, McIlroy hammed up a Texas accent. "What makes you so certain, Dr. d'Arbaud?"

"They know we are coming. They've known since, Jaeger, how long ago did mission control see our departure from Bravo Charlie orbit?"

Jaeger showed the palm of his free hand, asking her for patience, then queried his wearable through the subvocal microphone patches on his throat. The relativistic math was more complex than he wanted to do in his head. "Six months, give or take."

Six months for the inner parties of both factions to know, and plan. Only around now would civilian astronomers on Earth see *Napoleon*'s exhaust and realize it was not an anomaly from one of the stars of Alpha Centauri, nor long-mute *Concordia* coming home.

Marie said, "Every representative to each faction's high councils, and every insider pulling its strings, is planning to be someplace secluded at the time of our arrival."

"We can hit any place on Earth," Ulanovas said. He emphasized the words by popping a peppered beef-like cube into his mouth and chewing hard.

Annike put down her fork. Her free hand tugged on her ponytail. "But how would aliens know what those secluded places are?"

"Someone on the *Concordia* mission knew," Ulanovas said. He swallowed and his next words came clearly. "And the aliens got the intel out of them, okay?"

McIlroy's grimace scrunched up his beard. "We're pushing our luck if we go that way. If we go after targets that are too hidden, they might figure out who's really firing *Napoleon*'s guns at them."

"Same reason we can't selectively knock out the system-wide telescope network watching Bravo Charlie." Jaeger said. "So we hit only targets the aliens could guess at from orbit." He turned a reassuring smile to Annike. "There won't be many civilian deaths. If the higher-ups at all those targets sneak away, word will trickle down to the harmless and the innocent. They'll clear out too."

"And the weapons are precise enough?" She turned her brown eyes from him to Ulanovas and back.

"To the meter. The only places that will get damaged are the places I aim at."

She tugged her ponytail, then pulled her hand away and glanced at her slender fingers like she hadn't noticed what they'd done. "And if Earth hits back?"

"Impossible," said Ulanovas. He tore off a hunk of bread and plowed it through the pepper sauce.

Jaeger leaned back in his chair. His hand slipped away from Annike's and his gaze wandered through the gap between Ulanovas and McIlroy, into the depths of the rec room. Near the billiards and ping pong tables, a sitting area, where he and McIlroy had tried to get the others to play UltraHistory and been reduced to battling AIs. The computer players were generally weak, but still could play event cards to devastating effect.

"You sure about that? They've had six months to prepare for our arrival, and three-plus more to go."

"They try, and hit either the rock cap or a hull hardened against interstellar dust at relativistic speeds, okay? Even if they could pierce the hull, we could seal off ninety percent of the ship's interior space without harm to us."

"I reckon," McIlroy said, in a tone making clear he tried to convince himself.

Ulanovas shook out his sandy blond hair. "If any site shoots at us, we shoot back. They cannot release the focused power we can. So Earth might shoot at us. But only once."

Jaeger speared a crescent of onion, then jabbed his fork into a beef-like cube. He lifted the mouthful of food off his plate, and paused. "Maybe we want Earth to shoot at us."

Annike's brown eyes crinkled. "So we can shoot at more targets on Earth than we need to?"

"So we can pretend we suffered damage." He surveyed the table. No one followed him yet. "And some equipment separates from the ship and ends up in orbit."

"What sort of equipment?" McIlroy asked.

"A vacuum energy extractor and drive."

Her fingers around the stem of her wine glass, Marie pondered. "You want to give Earth the technology?"

"*Concordia*'s original purpose was to bring back knowledge for the benefit of all humankind," Jaeger said. "Vacuum energy would solve every energy crisis Earth has, from too much land given over to windmills and solar panels, to the high price of separating deuterium from hydrogen in sea water."

He went on. "Vacuum energy would also give Earth a better interstellar propulsion technology."

"Especially after we destroy the hydrogen collector at Jupiter," added McIlroy.

A hesitant note sounded in Annike's voice. "They'll come after us."

"We'll be safe on the ground on Bravo Charlie long before they do. Even more importantly, the stars will be in humankind's reach."

Ulanovas dropped his fork to his plate. "You propose we disassemble an extractor and a drive, then throw it overboard?"

"Something like that. We have enough of both to spare a set. So many telescopes will be watching us, everyone will see the equipment. It'll stay in orbit more than long enough for Earth to send a retrieval mission. And taking that kind of damage gives us an excuse to return to Bravo Charlie instead of staying in orbit and destroying ground targets." Jaeger looked at them all. "What am I missing?"

Annike spoke first. "Can you and Ulanovas remove an energy extractor and a drive?"

"We have the know-how."

"You'll have to cut a hole in the hull? Work in vacuum?"

"The suits Marie fabbed early on still hold up." He nodded in the direction of the Provençal woman.

Annike leaned back, clearly out of questions.

Ulanovas leaned forward. "We can do it. Though what if we use a laser to cut it loose but the only weapons Earth can throw at us are projectiles? They would know a kinetic impact would not slice through alloy the way a laser would. They would realize we dropped it intentionally. As if we gave them a gift."

"We'd have to plan for all the contingencies," Jaeger said, "then implement the one that looks best—"

"And it may not stay in orbit long enough, okay?"

"The extractor and drive burning up in the atmosphere wouldn't benefit anyone," McIlroy said.

Jaeger swiped away their objections with the back of his hand through the air, well above the level of their wine glasses. "I'll have to run the math on how long Earth would have to come up and retrieve it. But they'll have time."

"There's also the problem of it burning up in our exhaust beam, okay?"

"Maybe...." Jaeger drew out the word while his mind raced ahead. They would be best served by leaving Earth orbit before anyone came up for the extractor and drive. And their exhaust could destroy the equipment in an instant. "But we can avoid that by picking the right departure vector."

"That might give the game away too," McIlroy said.

"How so?" asked Annike.

"Military personnel handling advanced equipment are trained to keep it from falling into enemy hands. That's universal logic."

McIlroy ran the backs of his fingers over his bearded jaw. "If real aliens lost an energy extractor and drive, they'd vaporize them in the exhaust beam rather than let Earth grab them."

Silence descended over their corner of the rec room. Jaeger's gaze dropped to his nearly empty plate. His front teeth nibbled at his lower lip. Legitimate objections, sure, but they could overcome them.

"There's another problem," Marie said.

"What's that?" Jaeger's voice came out gruff. He cleared his throat and sipped wine to explain away his tone.

"Would the factions cooperate to retrieve the equipment? Or would they race to each seize it for itself?"

Jaeger's hand slumped from his wine glass to lie flat on the table. "That is a risk I hadn't thought of."

"Especially because they won't have earned it in battle, okay?" Ulanovas regarded them from under a loose sheaf of hair.

"Even if they cooperated enough to damage *Napoleon* and make it look like they knocked it off the ship...." McIlroy turned to Jaeger and raised his eyebrows in a look of confident gamesmanship, seen dozens of times across the UltraHistory table. "...how many times do allies win a war together, then turn into enemies when it comes time to divide the spoils?"

"The Humanist-Traditionalist cold war is an example," said Marie.

"The most recent example," McIlroy said.

"Oh. I always wondered what the English word *mansplaining* means. Now I know." She quirked her eyebrow but gave him a grin.

Tone light, McIlroy said, "I wouldn't have to, if you'd listen the first time."

Marie gave a gasp of mock outrage and lightly punched his upper arm.

Her boyfriend's voice grew serious. "But back to what we're talking about, I think the same thing would happen between Humanists and Traditionalists."

Her voice grew serious too. "One side gets vacuum energy weapons and destroys half the Earth."

Annike sounded even more solemn. "Or the side that loses the race decides that if it will be destroyed, it will bring down the other with the weapons of mass destruction both sides already have."

"You're right." Jaeger reached for her hand. He met her gaze, then looked to the others. He knew them better than members of his own family back on Earth. "All of you. I appreciate the sanity check."

"What friends are for," McIlroy said.

"It's settled. We scare the factions enough and make them mad enough to rebuild the hydrogen collector at Jupiter, build another ship—"

"Ships, I reckon."

"Mac, I bet you're right. A fleet of ships will come to Alpha Centauri to fight hostile aliens and save the survivors of the *Concordia* mission."

"Together," said Annike. "In peace."

Jaeger gave her a grin. "And best of all, spread as a unified species through the galaxy."

McIlroy reached for the plastic wine bottle in the center of the table. "Time to top off our glasses and toast to that."

CHAPTER 14

2 SEPTEMBER 2132

A COOL BREEZE from offshore rustled the dry grass atop the dunes. Leclerc's cropped tonsure of hair gave the breeze too little to work with. Waves lapped the verge of bare sand between the dunes and the ocean. A flock of small, pudgy birds patrolled the beach, hopping away from incoming waves, hopping back with sharp beaks at the ready to snatch whatever small and wriggly things the waves washed ashore for their breakfast.

Leclerc didn't know for sure whether the island belonged to North Germany or the Netherlands. Not that it mattered. North-western Europe was the most solidly Humanist bloc of territory on Earth. The borders between countries were lines on a map. A continuing legacy of the international cooperation born in the wake of the man-made disasters of two centuries ago.

Perhaps a harbinger of how the entire world could cooperate into the future.

Or that another man-made disaster could erupt at any moment? His mood dipped with the sand slumping under his shoes.

The sun, fat and low to his right, lit everything with cheery yellow rays. A few steps in front of Leclerc, the dawn sun glossed in Aggarwal's hair. Even the lighthouse ahead, its windows boarded over and the red and white stripes around its tower pitted by sand and storm, looked rustic instead of sinister.

They approached, through air leaving a thick salt tang in his nostrils. No guards, but cameras mounted over the door pivoted to track them. There were guns, too, Aggarwal had said, hidden in low casements in the grass, positioned to catch intruders between two jaws of fire. "But we'll be ID'd from the moment the boat docks."

The boat lay alongside the pier four hundred meters behind them, on the bayside, facing the mainland. Too distant to hear the squeak of the hull against the pier's bumpers. No escape if anything went wrong—

Leclerc drew in a breath. Nothing would go wrong.

At least for him, in the next hour.

They stopped at the door. It looked as weatherbeaten as the whitewashed wall next to it. The cameras watched them from the upper corners, each like a cyclops peering down its nose. Aggarwal knocked, four sharp raps. An electromagnetic lock released and the door swung inward, revealing a vestibule.

In they went. Lights came on in the ceiling, weak imitations of the morning sun. Walls in pallid white and trickles of sand on the floor near the entrance. More than enough room for them to stand in the middle of the vestibule, while the outer door swung shut and the inner one opened.

The scent of salty air faded in Leclerc's nose. The lighthouse interior dispelled the air of dilapidation. Two offices on either side of a hallway. Small spaces judging by how near the doors were to each other. All the doors were closed. Sounds of activity from inside, but Leclerc had no idea who worked in this place, or why.

The hallway had an open ceiling. Rising up the inside of the clapboard walls, a nanotube alloy skeleton reinforced the original wooden frame and held up a metallic stairway which wound around. The stairway was fully caged on bottom and sides, unlike the safety-hazard one at the Russian drydock. More offices cantilevered off the stairway, jutting into the interior. Windowless boxes all. The uppermost of the hanging offices seemed the most precarious. It hung near where the stairway ended at a door to the top level.

A guide arrow forced itself into Leclerc's vision. It pointed down the hallway until they reached a cross-corridor, then swung to the right. Past more closed offices, at the end of the corridor, an elevator with a single car waited with its door open.

He and Aggarwal followed the guide arrow in. The elevator door shut. It whisked them upward, fast enough that Aggarwal grunted and Leclerc reached for a waist-high grab bar to steady himself.

The elevator stopped at the top of the lighthouse. A single, circular room, with the last traces of salt scrubbed from the air. Video monitors ringed the inside of the boarded-up windows. Desks and control panels stood along the walls. Where the beacon and its assembly had once served sailors on treacherous seas, a round table topped in a pale, knotty wood. The table could seat a dozen, but was now in use by only two. As promised, Rubik and Memford. They sat with an empty chair between them.

Seeing only the people he'd expected to meet dialed down Leclerc's unease, but one notch only.

"Take some refreshment and sit, please," Rubik said. She extended a slender hand toward a side table between the elevator and the stairway door. "The coffee is actually quite good."

The side table held a coffee carafe, a pitcher of water, decanters with liquors. Leclerc poured himself a cup of coffee. A cautious sip proved her right. He waited as Aggarwal poured a finger of Scotch. The science bureaucrat then led the way to seats at the table, roughly opposite Memford and Rubik.

The American's T-shirt for today had some jagged letters with a lightning bolt down the middle. "Civilians have seen the alien ship," he said.

The blonde gave Leclerc a faint smile. "On the schedule you predicted."

"Who sighted it?"

"A university astronomy department in South India reported anomalous spectral features from Alpha Centauri," Memford said. "My people paid them a visit. Asked them to keep it under wraps. There's a sizable donation coming to them from London and Silicon Valley if they keep their mouths shut until we publicly announce the alien ship is coming."

Leclerc's hand cradled the coffee cup. "May I ask when that will be?"

"That's going to depend on what you can tell us, isn't it?"

Leclerc froze, except for a thick bob of his Adam's apple.

Rubik spoke. "Can we defeat the alien ship?"

A creak as Aggarwal shifted in his chair. He peered at Leclerc from under his bushy eyebrows.

Despite knots in Leclerc's stomach, he said, "We have to try."

"Was that our question?" Memford asked.

The knots tightened. "It should be." Leclerc blinked a few times. These people were not to be trifled with. Not even the blonde. "We believe this one ship is the only active alien presence anywhere in the galaxy."

Memford aimed his hatchet face at Leclerc. "We?"

More blinks. Don't mention the talk with Guo. "My science team at mission control."

"What leads you to that conclusion?" asked Rubik with a calm voice.

Leclerc's voice slowed down to match. "After a million years, exponential growth would have allowed the aliens to colonize every star system in the galaxy. That clearly failed to happen. We consider it likely that a disaster destroyed their homeworld shortly after they sent an expedition to Alpha Centauri. The expedition was not self-sufficient enough to turn into a permanent alien colony on Four Freedoms."

"They're extinct," mused Rubik.

"How do you know that?" asked Memford.

Leclerc met his gaze. "A million years of exponential growth would give the aliens enough time to fill the galaxy, whether they started with a population of a hundred or a hundred billion." Leclerc turned to Rubik. "We believe they converted their ship to automated control and put it into a dormant state, with instructions to wake if other civilizations explored the planet."

"Wake, I can see." Rubik's eyes crinkled. "But how would they know where the other civilization came from, to send their robotic ship?"

"The ship could easily scan nearby stars for radio transmissions. Earth emits a massive amount in all directions, and mission control has sent a steady stream of data to *Concordia* for years."

"Of course," she said. "My next question is, why would they code a robotic ship to do such a thing?"

"You know, out of spite." Aggarwal set down his empty glass with a thunk. "If they couldn't settle the galaxy no one else could either."

Leclerc shrugged. He'd mulled the question in what little downtime he had between trips to Russia, London, and Silicon Valley. "I do not know the purpose behind their mission. But if the ship has hostile intent, it's alone."

Rubik sucked in a breath. Her eyes lit up enough to tell Leclerc she jumped ahead to where his next words would go.

"If we defeat it," he said, "nothing else will stop us from spreading through the galaxy."

Memford brooded. "Stop us and the Trads, you mean."

"If we defeat one alien ship, we get only half the galaxy?" Rubik arched an eyebrow at Memford. "Are these odds good enough to push in all your chips?"

"We still don't know if we can defeat it," Memford said. "And with all the energy it can throw out its back end, it could sterilize the entire planet."

"Not all at once," she said. She checked a virtual display only she could see. "The laser systems from California can punch through a slab of metal four meters thick. The submarines have successfully hit target weather balloons at an altitude of sixty kilometers. Four submarines have already put to sea, with more coming out of the dock at a pace of three per month."

Memford crossed his arms in front of his T-shirt. "Fourteen subs by arrival day. *More* than enough."

She gave his sarcasm a jaundiced look. "We don't have to destroy the alien ship to defeat it. If we knock out its weapon systems, it cannot harm Earth."

"Unless it drives at full acceleration into the Atlantic between London and New York," Memford replied. "The shock wave and tsunami would be as big as the impact that killed off the dinosaurs."

"Still preferable to sterilizing the planet, is it not?" Her gaze speared Memford. "And it is more plausible that a damaged ship would retreat to Alpha Centauri rather than stay and risk destruction."

A glance between Memford and Aggarwal, then the latter spoke. "But, like, if it's a robotic ship, the aliens could have, you know, coded it to fight to the end. They're all dead. What do they care if their machines die too?"

Rubik ignored him. Her gaze remained on Memford. "If the aliens intended their robotic ship to destroy intelligent life at all costs, they would not have waited to send it out. They would have dispatched it on its mission as their dying act. They could not preclude the possibility that another civilization would reach Alpha Centauri after colonizing most of the galaxy. One robotic ship could not explore a hundred billion star systems and destroy a hundred billion worlds."

Memford looked unconvinced. "Or maybe the aliens think like aliens."

"If they are poor strategists," said Rubik, "then we have an even better chance of defeating their ship."

Memford sucked in a breath. His demeanor soon eased and he gave her a cold grin. "Poor strategists can be great tacticians. Just ask the Germans, right, Leclerc?"

He stammered, "I don't follow—"

Memford waved him off. "You're keeping your head down. Don't bother. You're a grinder and you believe there's some higher purpose to all your science crap. That's fine. We've learned from the past dictators, Hitler and Stalin and Mao and Wáng. We don't punish nobodies who sided with the old status quo when we set up a new one. Just keep following orders and no one will send you to a prison camp or an unmarked grave."

Leclerc's heart thudded in his chest. He could survive this. Sybil and Helene could survive this. "What are my orders?"

Memford leaned toward Leclerc. Lights in the ceiling caught the sharp angles of his face. "Send the message to the alien ship. Ask them to hit the Trads, let us go unscathed, and we'll never leave Sol system again."

"No," said Rubik. "We will uphold our alliance with the Traditionalists and resist the aliens together." Her graceful fingers brushed the tabletop, like a piano player at a soft passage of a piece by Chopin.

Memford whipped his head around. A smirk came to his lips. "We seem to be at an impasse." From the side of his mouth, he said, "Leclerc, you have your orders."

Rubik gave Memford a smile matching in its coldness. She jabbed two fingers at a knot in the wood. "Our impasse can be easily resolved. Osorio will cast the tiebreaking vote."

Behind Leclerc, the door unlocked with a mechanical click. It flew open, bouncing off a doorstop. Three men burst into the room, clad in dark suits bulky over bulletproof vests. They carried short rifles with magazines almost as long as the barrels. The muzzles swung up, one aimed at Aggarwal, the other two at Memford. "Hands up! Don't move!"

The two men raised their hands. Leclerc did the same. His heart hammered in his neck. His mouth tasted like a desert. All the moisture in his body had flooded his armpits and bulged his bladder.

Osorio, the gray man from the March meeting at Cheltenford Hall, spoke from behind the armed men. His voice, though soft, carried clearly through the room. "Not you, Leclerc. Get yourself clear." He pointed to a video display behind Rubik.

Leclerc lurched from his chair. He squatted below the muzzle aimed at Aggarwal and scrambled past it. He rose and ran, faster than he had in years. When he reached his destination, he sagged against the control panel and gulped breaths.

Memford ignored the armed men and Osorio. To Rubik, he said, "Set me up from the start, bitch?"

"Of course I did. I detest the Traditionalist leaders, but they're human. To side with aliens against our own species... any man who could seriously consider such a plan has abdicated any claim to be working for Humanist ideals."

"Humanist ideals? God damn, you say it like you believe it."

"I do." Rubik turned to Osorio. "Take them away."

"Gladly," he said, his voice as gray as his suit.

Aggarwal's bushy eyebrows jumped. The bloodshot whites of his eyes stood out against his swarthy face. "You were, like, listening?"

"We waited in the room below."

Eyes darting, Aggarwal said, "You heard Memford? You know, about the nobodies getting forgiven—"

"Who first proposed betrayal of the Traditionalists?" Osorio's soft voice and faint Latin accent covered but could not hide a threat.

"You've, like, got the wrong man!" Aggarwal waved a raised hand toward Leclerc, until Osorio's man adjusted his aim.

The soft voice replied, "I watched the recording of your prior meeting. I heard everything Leclerc said here today. He is the most innocent of all." Osorio's gaze met Leclerc's and he gave a little nod.

Leclerc's mouth worked, dry and silent. After a moment, he nodded back.

Osorio turned his attention to Memford and Aggarwal. "On the floor. Face down. Arms out. Do not move."

Memford did so, with a smirk on his face until the floor hid it. Aggarwal stood like a statue. One of the armed men slung his weapon, went behind Aggarwal, and kneed him in the backs of his legs. Aggarwal stumbled and teetered forward, raised arms wobbling. Osorio's man grabbed the sides of his torso and, with a grunt, lowered him to the floor. He swept together Aggarwal's hands and cuffed them behind the prisoner's back. He cuffed Memford next. The control lights on the handcuffs glowed as red as the eyes of tiny avenging angels.

"Move," Osorio said. His man who'd worked the cuffs helped Memford, then Aggarwal, to their feet. Aggarwal kept glancing over his shoulder at the muzzle leveled on the middle of his spine. Memford gave one final look at Rubik and Leclerc, smirk still on his face, then turned and started for the door.

After Osorio, his men, and the prisoners left, the door swung shut. The circular room felt too large. Too quiet, with only the hum of fans and Leclerc's catching breath.

His gaze landed on the door. "What's to happen to them?"

"They will be rehabilitated," Rubik said. Her tone was sweet and light. He probed it for lies but could not find any as she went on. "After a few years at a science station on the Antarctic coast."

"Without a radio transmitter that can reach orbit."

"Precisely." Her smile showed teeth. "They will not trouble us in our joint defense against the aliens. Come, sit." She beckoned at the chair next to her, tucked against the table between her and the one spun out and vacated by Memford.

The chair rolled out for him. He waited until it moved back, where he could rest his forearms on the table for support. He'd never been this close to someone who wielded so much power. And seemed so calm in the aftermath of its use. "Will we continue to keep the public in the dark?"

"Should we?"

"No. They deserve to know what is coming. We need not say the alien ship is hostile, but if we admit to not knowing its intentions, that will be enough for people to plan."

"And?"

"We should announce we work with the Traditionalists in preparing our defenses. Though we can't give particulars."

"And if we publicize our joint defense with the Trads, word will get to the Trad public and military personnel. The Trad leaders would lose a great deal of credibility with their people if they sided with aliens against us." She smiled. Her perfume was some delicate aroma he could only afford for Sybil on milestone anniversaries. "Well done."

"I didn't propose it to hamstring the Traditionalist leadership."

"I know you didn't." She turned to open space above the table and gestured. An icon and chime in Leclerc's senses told him she wanted to share a virtual workspace.

He accepted the shared channel as she said, "How exactly shall we announce the alien ship to the world?"

Leclerc hesitated, but only for a moment. "Perhaps we should prepare our announcement together with our new allies."

CHAPTER 15

8 SEPTEMBER 2132 (EARTH REFERENCE FRAME) | 11 NOVEMBER 2128 (*NAPOLEON* REFERENCE FRAME)

JAEGER'S SHIRT and pants slid along the crawlspace floor, snug against his belly and thighs. His feet probed behind him as he wriggled backward, toward the access panel and the corridor circling the engineering deck where he could stand up straight. He shifted his head between a neutral position, brim of hard hat scraping the crawlspace floor near the white blob from his head lamp, to his neck craned back and the lamp lighting up the equipment in his his outstretched hands.

He tugged a pair of defective extractor plates, bound together in their housing. The thin but heavy and rigid slab could only slide down the crawlspace at an angle, one long side in the lower left corner, the other in the upper right. Each bend in the crawlspace required an extra yank to move the plate housing. Alloy shrieked, louder than his grumbled curses, as the housing moved an inch.

Jaeger gulped dry and warm air, and regretted his curses. Thank your higher power the vacuum energy extractors had such big parts. The Octaliens had been so small that if they'd sized the extractor maintenance crawlspaces just big enough for their bodies, no human being could squeeze in. The crawlspace structure lacked the shape-changing alloys the Octaliens used elsewhere, in part because equipment packed the volume around the crawlspace. *Napoleon*'s crew would've been forced to do repairs by robot, or rip apart the extractors and attendant hardware and hope they could put the puzzle pieces back together again.

Crawling backwards would do well enough.

Another tug. He wormed his body flat. The toes of his boots skipped along the crawlspace floor, then came to air.

Finally. Almost out—

The shipwide radio channel crackled to life in his earbuds. Annike said, "Everyone. We've picked up a broadcast from Earth."

Excited chatter over the channel. Jaeger's heart thumped. "Not a message to us?"

"No," Annike said. "But important all the same."

He grabbed the extractor plate housing and gave another tug. "I've almost pulled the old unit, then I need to put the new one in. Can we talk about it when I'm up there for lunch?"

"I reckon we can wait," McIlroy said. The shipwide channel fell silent.

Silent, with only the hum of the fifteen online drives coming to Jaeger's ears and seeping into his body. But his racing thoughts echoed in his mind. They'd considered Earth might send them message, though with a lot of debate whether it would be a challenge, a negotiation, or a surrender. McIlroy had suggested one or both of the factions might try to ally with the incoming 'alien' ship against the other. Which seemed too cynical, even for a master UltraHistory player—

Jaeger stood in the corridor outside the access panel, with two extractor plate housings leaning against the wall near his feet. A sour feeling curdled in his stomach. Which was the defective unit he'd pulled, and which the replacement?

He tipped the one on his left away from the wall, saw his handwritten word *bad* in grease pen, and relaxed.

Focus on the repair, then let your mind wander about what Earth might have broadcast.

An hour later, extractor and drive operational, stomach grumbling, he made his way up a ladderway toward the deck the five of them occupied. On narrow landings from the top of one ladder to the bottom rung of the next, he passed dark corridors. Entire decks, most of the ship, reconnoitered in the weeks orbiting Bravo Charlie and abandoned for three years. The final climb, toward light and the aromas of roasted onions and beefy protein, seemed the fastest of all.

He was the last to reach the rec room. Ulanovas, McIlroy, and Marie d'Arbaud sat at the table, steaming plates in front of them and water or diet cola in their cups. Annike gave him a smile. "All is good?"

"The drive is ready. I want to get it online soon. The other fifteen can keep up our deceleration, but the more power we push through them—" He read her expression and shook his head. "After lunch. And after you show us what you picked up from Earth."

He followed her through the kitchenette, heaping the hydroponic onions and fabbed fake meat onto his plate, adding a burst of greens and a pour of balsamic vinaigrette.

They joined the others at the table. Ulanovas took a bite, jaws mashing his food. McIlroy said to Annike, "Now that we're all here, don't keep us waiting."

"Certainly," Annike said. She put down her fork, tapped and swiped air.

A video frame appeared in the air in front of Jaeger. A glance at the others showed a virtual window appeared for all of them in the same relative location.

Then he refocused on the image.

A balding man, graying hair and a neat mustache. A Chinese

woman in a dark blue skirt-suit and a half-jade yin-yang pendant at her neck.

"That's Leclerc," Annike said. "Director of mission control. I don't know the woman by name."

McIlroy's eyes narrowed. "A Traditionalist, I reckon." To Marie: "Recognize her?"

She shook her head, then glanced in turn at Ulanovas and Jaeger. "Do you?"

Jaeger squinted at a spot near the ceiling. "Zhou? Gao? Guo." He met their gazes. "She's from the science directorate in St. Petersburg."

"Someone from each faction," Marie said.

An excited edge to her normally calm voice, Annike said, "Look at the backdrop."

Frozen in the video frame, Leclerc and Guo stood in front of a blue drapery, on which hung a circular seal. The words *International Interstellar Exploration Agency - Joint Commission on Alien Affairs* ringed a logo. It resembled the IIEA's original logo, modified with two human outlines aiming a telescope at a single bright dot in a deep blue sky.

A telescope, or a weapon?

"Play it, babe," Jaeger said.

Annike nodded. The video came to life. Some frames splotchy, some staticky, the sound at times dropping out for a second or two. Received, filtered from the radio frequency roar of the drives, and amplified, over distances so vast, amazing they could see and hear anything at all.

"An alien ship departed Alpha Centauri approximately five years ago," Leclerc said. His French accent was thicker than Marie's. "At relativistic speeds on a flight path to Sol system, to Earth. The light from its departure and travel reached the IIEA's telescope array a few months ago. After we ruled out other phenomena, and after ground-based observers corroborated our data, we realized the need to work together, to share the news with all the peoples of Earth."

He shuffled back. Guo shifted closer to center stage. "We know or strongly believe several things about the alien ship. It did not silence *Concordia*. The IIEA vessel ceased transmissions long before the alien ship left for Earth. We do not believe it is the reason *Concordia* is delayed in starting its return voyage, for the same reason."

"Can't tell if she's lying," muttered McIlroy.

Marie nudged his shoulder with hers. "Shh."

The fork in Jaeger's hand came to his awareness. The morning's work on the engineering deck made his stomach rumble. He jabbed his fork at an onion sliver and a protein chunk.

"—alien civilization capable of building the ship would be visible to Earth," Guo said, "just as ours would be visible to such a civilization on Bravo Charlie. We saw no sign of an alien civilization on the planet twenty years ago, when IIEA came together to plan the *Concordia* expedition. The expedition—" Garbled voice and image. "—no report—alien civilization on the planet. We believe the ship to be a robotic craft originating from an alien civilization from outside the Alpha Centauri system."

Ulanovas spoke around a mouthful of salad. "They make some good guesses, okay?"

In the video window, Leclerc spoke. "We believe it comes with a peaceful intent." His gaze darted to something or someone to the side and out of camera view. "The vast distances of interstellar travel make the conquest of another species far too expensive for any mind to attempt it, no matter how alien."

"Those vast distances, in combination with the capabilities we presume it has," Guo said, "mean there are no raw materials or finished products worth seeking in trade." She spoke smoothly, plainly more accustomed than Leclerc to speaking to large public audiences.

Or to lying?

"—peaceful discussions." Guo said. "*Concordia* may be irreparably damaged and it brings home our lost ship's personnel. It may be that it comes to help us meet its masters elsewhere in interstellar space."

Leclerc mashed his lips together for a fleeting moment. After the expression vanished, he took over, "Together, we have prepared and will continue to prepare for the alien ship's arrival at Earth. That momentous day will come in about three months. And together, we will—" His image froze, jump-cut. "—all mankind."

After a pause, Guo's dark eyes scanned over what Jaeger guessed were reporters standing behind and near the camera. "We will take questions."

They started off easy. How long had it been seen, had they talked to it, had it talked to them. Leclerc and Guo took turns answering, based on whose part of the speech the question related to. A few months, no, no.

What preparations? Teams of contact personnel, training in Houston, to be launched from Baikonur once the alien ship invited them to visit it in orbit.

"How can you be certain the alien ship comes in peace?" a bland American voice. "What if they don't want to conquer Earth, but destroy it, so we're never a threat to them?"

Leclerc's mouth gaped like a fish in a boat. Guo leaned forward. "The idea that the galaxy is so crowded, and so easily colonized, that civilizations would inevitably exterminate one another for it is a paranoid belief. Let us leave it on the ash heap of history with the Wáng regime. Next?"

The questions petered out after that. Guo and Leclerc left the scene. The camera zoomed out, showed a crowd of milling reporters, as a male voice with a crisp British accent summarized what they'd just—

Annike snapped her fingers. The image froze and fell silent in front of Jaeger. "What do we think?"

A wry grin showed amid McIlroy's brown beard. "Annihilation might be paranoid, and Guo might not want to talk about it, but that doesn't mean she thinks its impossible."

Jaeger nodded. "You saw Leclerc's eyes when he said they wouldn't come to conquer? It was a giveaway."

"The conquest talk was a red herring," said McIlroy. "Aliens wouldn't come to Earth to conquer it. Anybody in the know could see that."

Eyebrow arched at him, Marie replied, "They weren't talking to people who know better. They were talking to reporters."

Chuckles and smiles went around the table. The first face to grow sober was Jaeger's. "If they know us 'alien robots' could be coming with hostile intent, what kind of preparations are they making?"

"Weapons platforms?" McIlroy looked thoughtful. "Orbital or ground based?"

"You still worry about this?" Ulanovas swept back a lock of hair. "They cannot harm us, and if they try, we destroy the weapons platforms, okay?"

Jaeger propped his chin on his fist and gave the pilot a firm look. "Yeah. I am going to worry about it."

Ulanovas rolled his eyes.

"Leclerc and Guo are trying to keep the masses on Earth from panicking about us 'alien death robots.' Right?"

Around the table, faces showed agreement.

Jaeger went on. "But I bet they took into account us picking up the broadcast. If they think we have hostile intent, they aren't going to say, 'we're going to use satellites or twentieth century missile silos as platforms to strike back.'"

"They'll assume we can understand English," McIlroy said, nodding.

"Or a civilized language," chimed in Marie, a playful smile on her thin lips. Then her gaze met Jaeger's and her smile faded.

He aimed his attention back at Ulanovas. "We need to tweak the plan. Here's why."

"Why?"

"Jupiter isn't on our straight line to Earth."

"I've looked at the same charts as you, okay?"

"Our current plan is to strike the hydrogen collector while decelerating, then change our vector to enter Earth orbit. How much time to get from Jupiter to Earth?"

Ulanovas squinted at a virtual display. "Three days." He corrected himself. "Little more."

"If they've developed weapons platforms, we give them three days to shoot at us before we reach orbit. While we can't return fire, because we're backing up and our main lasers are mounted on the front and sides."

A glum look came to Ulanovas's face. "When we back up, we show them the most vulnerable parts of the ship."

"The parts that would get us away from vengeful Earth," McIlroy said.

Annike waggled a forkful of salad in the air. "But it is important to hit the hydrogen collector, isn't it?"

Ulanovas' face switched to a grin. "I can hit it from Earth orbit."

Her brown eyes regarded him. "From, what's the distance, five hundred million kilometers?"

"I can swat a fly at twice that range," he said. "The hydrogen collector is a big target, easy to damage without hitting the crew capsule at the outer end, okay?"

"But it would take a laser beam, what, half an hour to cross that distance?"

"I will lead the hydrogen collector. Is not a problem. It cannot see the laser coming, okay? It cannot dodge."

Jaeger curled his fingers around his water cup. "Half an hour to hit the hydrogen collector. Half an hour for the skeleton crew at the collector to get word back to Earth. We spend that hour hitting targets on the ground."

"We won't even have to stay," Ulanovas said. "Destroy the sites we've chosen, send a message that next time will be even worse for them, and leave."

"Three subjective years in flight, and we stay in orbit a few hours?" Marie said.

McIlroy turned to her. "The best time to leave will be right after we take hostile action. Just in case they shoot back."

Jaeger spoke. "We need some time in orbit before we fire the guns. Extractor and drive maintenance. We're frying extractor plates at an increasing rate, especially on numbers three and four. I want to overhaul those two and run full diagnostics on everything else."

"What's the worst case if we don't?" Annike asked.

"Absolute worst? We accelerate away, lose all the drives, and coast at a fraction of light-speed forever." He raised a hand to calm everyone. "Before it gets that bad, let's say if we lose half the drives, we'd have to lower our acceleration and deceleration to reduce wear and tear on the ones we have left."

"Why would that be a problem?"

Ulanovas nodded toward the air, where the video had just played. "They could catch us before we return to Alpha Centauri."

Annike arched an eyebrow at that. "Even if we destroy the hydrogen collector?"

Voice raised, Jaeger replied. "We're here to force Earth to unite against an alien threat. If we do our job right, the first thing the Trads and Humanists will do together is fix it."

CHAPTER 16

13 DECEMBER 2132

Leclerc had been away from mission control far too long. Too many little things had changed, from Evans giving him an awkward smile from behind the desk in his former office to the stuffed chimera on the ledge of the horseshoe, which now gave a gimlet eye to a toy alien of green plastic skin, bulging skull, and laser pistol in its right hand.

The big board had changed too. Bravo Charlie had been shunted to the lower left corner. A tiny dot, glowing in infrared, crawled across it, a sign that mute *Concordia* remained in orbit. As of about forty months ago, when photons of its life support system's waste heat started the journey to Earth.

The alien robotic ship wanted to deny the galaxy to humankind. Everyone here at mission control understand that, from the lowest ranking techs, through people like Broaddus, Tung, Wojniakowski, and Yasmina Khan, through Hagerty behind him in the horseshoe, up to Guo and him and the people above them in the Traditionalist and Humanist hierarchies.

So why hadn't it annihilated *Concordia* in a moment, instead of letting the human ship remain in orbit?

He turned his attention to the main screen, though he knew in his bones the image there would not answer his question.

A thick hockey puck of a ship. Over a kilometer across, but the ship itself gave no sense of scale. The array of telescopes, members positioned from the leading and trailing Trojan asteroids of Jupiter to a dancing Lissajous orbit above the south pole of the sun, provided three-dimensional detail. Sixteen beams of light, hot and bright as the depths of a star, emerged in a ring from the rear of the ship as it backed toward Earth orbit.

Hot and bright but not uniform. The telescopes picked up fluctuations in power output from two adjacent drives. Milliseconds later, the other fourteen tweaked their output to keep the ship on its vector of constant deceleration.

It crossed the asteroid belt now. In seventy-two hours, its vector would put it fifteen hundred kilometers over Earth, orbiting at 25,000 klicks per hour.

It would not try to land. If it came to devastate Earth's cities, Humanist and Traditionalist alike, it had no need to descend to the surface. A combination of pitch, roll, and yaw, followed by a brief burn of its engines to a higher orbit, and it would leave a trail of devastation that would make the great firestorms of past wars, Dresden and Tokyo, Mumbai and Beijing, look like children playing with matches.

Leclerc sipped coffee and leaned back against the horseshoe. The people working behind him did not complain. His gaze roved the views from the individual telescopes, looking from every angle at the alien ship.

A cap of rusty red rock on the front, stained with a dull palette of grays and blacks. A shield against interstellar dust, when the ship had accelerated toward Earth. Hatches on the sides. What might pop out of those? Radio antennas?

Laser beams?

He studied one of the hatches. If a weapon emerged from it, the laser submarines would have a target.

They'd proven Memford wrong. Fifteen subs, not fourteen, had slipped out of the dock. The most recent one hit the water yesterday. Crews picked from the best personnel of all the world's navies. After the September broadcast, followed by word trickling down chains of command to the effect of *the scientists think they come in peace, but just in case,* more sailors had volunteered than the defense fleet could use.

Blended crews, hurried training. Each weapon passed a full power test at a gunnery range in the California desert prior to shipment to the drydock. Each crew passed target practice, using pointer lasers barely powerful enough to pierce the atmosphere to paint a sensor on a satellite rushed into orbit.

Would it be enough?

Distantly behind him, a door thumped shut. He glanced over his shoulder. Guo came into the room, alone. In a slim dress of deep maroon, under a brown leather overcoat, she made her way between workstations and past the glass-walled meeting room. The control room held the same cavernous chill as it had every other winter. A cluster of men in military uniforms—Russian navy, air force of the Pacific States of America, others unfamiliar to Leclerc—lifted buzz-cut heads as she passed, then hunched back over their boards, refocused on their work.

Guo carried a cup of coffee. Steam from it rose past the pendant at her neck. Jade and porcelain, yin and yang, coming together. Which half were the Traditionalists and which the Humanists?

He jittered his head to shake off idle musing. The factions had come together. The aliens had given them a common cause for the first time since Wáng the tyrant. Like something out of an UltraHistory game.

Leclerc frowned at his coffee cup. UltraHistory, who had

mentioned it? Memford, that was it, when he plotted to conspire with the aliens against the Traditionalists.

He sipped coffee. At least one of the changes around mission control had been for the good. Someone had replaced the coffeemaker in the break room with one that produced a drinkable beverage instead of a charred sludge. Warmth spread through his chest, melting away his foolish feeling.

A rustle of movement from inside the horseshoe. "Leclerc, Hagerty, Evans, everyone, good morning," Guo said.

Leclerc turned. Her dark eyes roved the array of screens. "Do we have visual on the hydrogen collector?" she asked.

"We'll call that up," Hagerty said. He muttered something to Broaddus. Keys clacked. Images flickered on the big board. "There. Middle right."

The main body of the collector station showed as a gray oblong against the red and yellow bands of Jupiter. The station rode in a precarious orbit around the planet, uneasily balanced at the L1 point between Io and the gas giant. The camera picked up the blinking nav beacons on the crew compartment on the end facing away from Jupiter. Only a skeleton crew, all volunteers, remained on the station now. They'd evacuated the rest two weeks ago.

As they watched, a puff of fusion fire kept the station at its intended orbit. The carbon nanotube umbilicus, snaking like an elephant's trunk almost half a million kilometers to the planet's atmosphere, was far too slender to be seen.

"All looks normal," Leclerc said.

At his position inside the horseshoe, Broaddus nodded. "Collector ops report the same thing."

Guo's voice turned thoughtful. "The alien ship did not fire on it. Why?"

Hagerty took off his video glasses and cleaned them on the hem of his sweater. What was left of his red-brown hair remained plastered to scalp. "Maybe they didn't recognize it as a fueling station for inter-stellar ships?"

"That seems implausible," Guo said.

Hagerty quailed. He slipped his glasses back on and slunked toward the exit to the horseshoe. "Just a thought."

A squeak of a rotating chair. Broaddus adjusted the gold clasp of his necktie. "They know Connie used a Bussard ramscoop to get to Bravo Charlie. They know Connie would need a boost to get fast enough to fuel herself off deep space hydrogen. But that doesn't mean they would recognize the collector as something we need for that."

Leclerc gave his head a slow shake. "Even if whatever intelligences aboard that ship don't recognize the collector as part of our interstellar mission infrastructure, they will realize it has industrial significance for our operations in space. Assuming they intend to stop us from any such operations, they would target it."

"Mr. Leclerc has it," Guo said mildly.

The activity of the workers across the large room gave a background rustle. Evans spoke over it. "They come in peace after all?"

"No," Leclerc said. "What did *Concordia* do when first it arrived at Bravo Charlie? Maintenance. Repairs. Intelligence gathering on where to deploy the Glenn and Yang ground expeditions. Presumably more planning for the xenology expedition. The aliens would do the same."

"And take no hostile action until they finished," Guo added.

"They're going to hit the collector on their way out Sol system?" asked Broaddus.

Guo shook her head. "We're a decade away from testing a laser propulsion system that could hit a smaller target at ten times the distance. The alien ship should have no problem destroying the hydrogen collector from Earth orbit, if it chooses."

Arched eyebrows and a flash of orange-brown palms. Broaddus asked, "Why wouldn't it?"

She gave a puzzled frown. After a moment, her expression changed, presumably after considering his question in the context of her previous words. "Oh, I expect it will."

Hagerty swiped his palms down his sweater over his hipbones. "Makes perfect sense. We should have seen it ourselves."

Guo's gaze remained on the hydrogen collector, then shifted to the decelerating alien ship. It did not seem to move against the backdrop of stars.

"If they won't take hostile action for a while," Evans said, "should we strike first?"

"No," Leclerc and Guo said at about the same time.

She looked over the ledge at Leclerc, a faint smile on her lips. "Are we supposed to say to one another, 'jinx'?"

Leclerc shrugged. "Ask the Americans. It's their folkway, not a French one."

Evans chuckled. Hagerty cracked a nervous smile, which soon gave way to a questioning look. "If we strike first, we get the advantage of surprise. Given the aliens's superior technology—"

"We would lose moral legitimacy in the public eye," said Leclerc. The conversation around the dinner table the night before came back to him. Helene, his daughter, seventeen now, believed with full innocence the words he'd uttered in the September broadcast. "We told the world the aliens come in peace."

"We can always tell them we picked up signs of aggressive intent," Hagerty said. "Or that we lied in our first broadcast to throw the aliens off the scent."

"It's also possible," Guo said, "we have misjudged the intent of the —what word did you use, Mr. Leclerc?"

"Intelligences?"

She pressed her palms together and gave him a little bow. "The intelligences crewing the ship."

"Though we doubt it," Leclerc said. He gave Guo a second glance. *Don't we?*

"Yes, the economic logic of interstellar travel is stark," Guo said. "There is another advantage to waiting till the aliens strike first. Even after London and St. Petersburg decided to work together for joint defense, there was an informal power bloc within the Traditionalist leadership that plotted to ally with the aliens against the Humanist Alliance." She gave Leclerc a wry smile. "You were fortunate to avoid a comparable attempted treason against humanity."

She knew the story of Memford and Aggarwal's scheme as well as he did. Perhaps his time with her had made him comfortable with lying. Or his exposure to his former colleagues had done it? "Fortunate indeed."

"Luckily, I and other Traditionalists arrested the conspirators before they could damage our joint defense effort. But there may be others, and I daresay in London no less than St. Petersburg, who would exploit an opportunity to use the aliens to gain an advantage over the other of the Coalition and the Alliance."

Knitted brows. Shared glances of puzzlement. She spoke too elliptically for the scientists around her.

"If the aliens strike targets of both factions," Leclerc said, "then the battle lines are clear. Them versus humankind."

On the ledge, the hard plastic alien still aimed its blaster at the stuffed, floppy chimera. Leclerc's gaze rose, carried on the wave of expressions on faces both inside and outside the horseshoe. All eyes went to the big board, to the alien ship filling the large and central view.

"What do we do till then?" Evans asked.

Guo cleared her throat. Leclerc let her answer. "The thing that is both simplest and hardest. We wait."

In the afternoon, three days later, within five seconds of the time calculated by Leclerc and Guo's people in mission control, the alien ship cut its engines. It floated two thousand kilometers above the Atlantic Ocean, seven latitude degrees north of the equator, in an orbit that took it over Europe in ten minutes and around the world in two hours.

The masses in the cities below looked up. The glinting dot sailed through the sky. People watched virtual displays, projected on the curve from wall to ceiling of subway cars or hovering in automobile cabins. Zoomed ground-based images of the alien ship, a more detail than the naked eye, its thick disc shape and rock cap apparent. News readers with choked voices described the historical moment.

The alien ship took no action. The news readers repeated themselves, merely filling up air time, describing a vessel the people of Earth could see for themselves. The glinting dot coasted along its orbit and soon went out of sight.

The masses minimized their virtual displays, turned on breaking news notifications, and continued with their daily lives. Students like Leclerc's daughter Helene crammed for end-of-term exams. Delivery robots lowered parcels containing wrapped gifts to front steps. Shoppers at Christmas markets cradled bags of hot roasted chestnuts in their gloved hands. The alien ship receded from their minds.

The masses did not notice when government officials left early for their winter holidays.

The masses did not notice the submarines, under the ocean at cruising depth, tracking the alien ship with help from the military personnel working at mission control.

Jaeger still hated free fall. His stomach flopped. Heartburn crawled up his throat and his genitals wanted to hide inside his body. Instead of cups and plates and eating around a table, like friends should, they squirted water and wine from squeezebulbs into their mouths, and did the same with protein goo like reddish toothpaste, while drifting around the kitchenette.

He'd hoped free fall would make his repair work easier, but even though they were weightless, the extractor plate pairs and control units still had mass. Unlike *Concordia*'s few people rated for exterior repairs, he hadn't trained in scuba gear in a neutral buoyancy tank. He repaired systems he had less familiarity with, repaired damage he hadn't seen before, like the control circuit fried by a burst of cosmic rays through extractors three and four.

How many cosmic rays had bombarded the DNA in the cells of his body? Unify Earth, then die of cancer before you get back to Alpha Centauri....

He continued his work. Tools, disconnected fasteners, and flakes of alloy corroded by years of intense energies wanted to squirm away, only to come back and jab him in the arm or drop a speck of dust into his eye.

Slower than he wanted, a week all told, Jaeger got the repairs done. Up—no longer *up* in free fall, of course, but he knew what he meant. Back on their deck, he zipped up the shower and slid the wand controls from soap to rinse to wet-vac. Dry and out, he pulled on a clean jumpsuit. He pulled himself hand-over-hand from one grab bar to the next through the corridors to the rec room.

McIlroy and d'Arbaud brushed their shoulders and legs together in the kitchenette in the corner, around the warm smells of Marie's cooking and the hum and beep of the microwave. She favored Jaeger with a smile on her thin lips. "The engines are ready?"

"They'll get us back to Alpha Centauri." And hopefully, a few years after that, back to Earth. After the factions united, and their joint task force returned the alien ship to the homeworld as a prize.

"You couldn't have timed the repairs any more perfectly," said McIlroy.

"How so?"

McIlroy's eyes glinted above his beard. "Check the calendar."

A puzzled squint at him, then Jaeger checked the date. "24 February 2129."

"Not ours. Earth's."

Shoulders tense, stomach growling, what did time dilation have to do with it? Jaeger swiped through menus. "Tuesday, 23 December 2132—" His voice brightened. "Almost Christmas."

"Exactly. Aliens won't know holidays from Thursdays, but government facilities will be closed."

"Fewer civilian and low-level casualties. The best time to strike." Jaeger rubbed his chin. "While it would have been good to hit the movers and shakers, they've cowered in secret bunkers for the last week. We weren't going to hit them, no matter what."

Motion at the door. Jaeger turned. Annike, a thoughtful look on her face. In free fall, his momentum kept him spinning. He ratcheted his gaze back to her each time he spun too far. Locking his view on her helped keep his stomach from rising any farther than it already had.

"Babe," he said on one pass, followed by, "What's up?"

"Did I hear you correctly? You're planning to strike on Christmas? You need not wait."

He'd held out his arms to slow his rotation and build up drag in the air long enough to come to a stop. "What do you mean?"

"I've monitored signals from the surface all afternoon. Both faction headquarters have granted their employees three days leave, starting tomorrow, the 24th. They are not to return until Monday the 29th. Most national and subnational governments have followed the lead of St. Petersburg and London."

Jaeger grinned at her, then broadened his expression to include McIlroy and Marie. "What's a more evil thing for aliens to do? Attack Earth on Christmas Eve, or Christmas Day?"

Chuckles and smiles. Warmth bubbled in Jaeger's chest. The plan really would work. The factions would set aside their differences and come to Alpha Centauri in pursuit. By the time they learned the truth of the false flag attack, the old labels, Traditionalist or Humanist, would lie forgotten.

It would make it worthwhile, to be now so close to Earth but unable to go home to it.

Voice light, McIlroy said to Annike, "Pick up any other signals from the ground?"

"The IIEA alien affairs team sent another greeting message. This time they added video clips of classrooms full of school children from around the world." Her tone turned wistful, then muted. "Saying in unison *welcome friends.*"

Jaeger drifted toward her, put his arm around her shoulders.

"What's going on?" He touched his lips to her clean blond hair. "Those children are hundreds or thousands of miles out of the line of fire. They'll be fine. And better off when the factions aren't stock-piling weapons of mass destruction to use against each other."

She raised her hand to his chest. The internal crawling sensations of free fall abated a little. "I know. No, it's... seeing Earth. Seeing children. My contraceptive implant will run out soon, but to have a child here, or on Bravo Charlie, if it isn't too late...."

After a moment, she shook her head. Her ponytail whipped through the air. She turned clear brown eyes to him. "Now isn't the time to talk about such things. But on our way back to Alpha Centauri?"

He leaned his head away to get a full look at her, then squeezed her closer and rested his cheek against a taut sheaf of her silky hair. "First thing."

Low whistling came from the hallway. Annike disentangled from him. He pivoted. McIlroy and Marie shared a look of emotional connection. They dialed it back and put some distance between themselves.

Ulanovas tugged himself into the rec room. He surveyed the four of them, then rolled his eyes. "You can be couples around me, okay?"

"We were talking about striking tomorrow or the next day," Jaeger said.

"Christmas," McIlroy added. "Down there."

Ulanovas considered, then shrugged. He spoke with ease. "Say the word. I've tracked all the targets. Easy to hit them as we fly over. The hydrogen collector requires more precise timing, can we see Jupiter from our place in orbit and where is Io in its orbit of Jupiter? But the circumstances will align often enough."

Jaeger said, "You seem confident."

"I've pored over old maps and current observations. Cross-refer-enced to data flows Annike has picked up. I found no weapons emplacements that can harm us, okay?"

"Are you sure?"

Under his sandy blond bangs, Ulanovas rolled his eyes. "We can see any ballistic missile coming at us in time for *Napoleon*'s defensive lasers to neutralize it. For a laser or other beam weapon to have any chance of piercing the hull requires a power source so large we could see it from up here. A fission reactor is difficult to hide. Especially if it is close to a laser station. I didn't see such a thing."

Jaeger shared a look with the others. They'd agreed on this plan in Bravo Charlie orbit years ago. A glance showed each one of them remained committed. There was risk, of the deaths of civilians and innocent employees in the faction headquarters ending up on their consciences. But the reward could be the peaceful spread of humankind across the galaxy. "We're ready to do this."

A wry head shake from McIlroy. A smile touched Marie's soft eyes. "There is one more thing we should do tonight."

"Which is?" Jaeger asked.

She twisted in the air. McIlroy nudged her shoulder and she sailed toward the refrigerator. She steadied herself with one on the side, the other on the door handle. Keeping her position, she opened the refrigerator and reached in.

One at a time, she pulled out squeezebulbs and tossed each toward one of her friends. "It was one Atrocious Wine Day the night before *Napoleon* left for Earth. Let tonight be another."

CHAPTER 17

24 DECEMBER 2132

THE SERVING dishes of his family's Christmas Eve dinner spread across the cream-colored linen tablecloth. Near the center lay a goose breast with crispy browned skin, butterflied and stuffed with a chestnut paste. Color popped from a serving bowl of blanched green beans, a dish of yellow-gold butter, and glasses of a mild red wine. Polished silverware gleamed next to fine porcelain. Three candle flames fluttered, accenting the half-dimmed light from the ceiling.

The dining room was a bubble of light and warmth against the darkness of the wintry late afternoon reigning outside the curtained windows.

Leclerc sat at the head of the table. The tablecloth's knotted end brushed his knees. He breathed a symphony of aromas into his nose and mouth. He gave a warm look to Helene to his left, then a longer and warmer one to Sybil on his right. "The meal looks wonderful. I wish I could have done more to help—"

"You opened and poured the wine," she said. Had her voice lost a little of its sparkle this year? The wrinkles on her face grown longer and deeper?

Probably, yes... and he looked into her brown eyes and did not care.

"And we know you are busy, Papa, with the alien ship." Helene had dyed her hair bright red during the months he'd been traveling. He still hadn't gotten used to this latest sign she grew up. "Did a message come in? Is that what kept you in your study all day?"

"No."

Her eyes turned soft. She had a kind soul, and God willing it would remain after she grew up more and life crumbled her innocence. "Is there something wrong—"

"Hush." He put his palms together and bowed his head. "First, grace."

Sybil and Helene mirrored his movements. He spoke, perfunctory words to a generic higher power, and because he was a loyal employee of the multinational Humanist hierarchy, no mention of Christ.

"Amen," they echoed.

Ladles and spoons clanked on serving plates. Sybil apologized for not cooking a whole goose and Leclerc assured her they had more than enough food for the three of them.

Helene said, "I wish we could have visited Uncle Martin in Paris this year."

Visit a target zone? Leclerc glanced at Sybil before answering their daughter. "I'm very busy, dear one, and must stay close to mission control."

"That makes sense," Helene said, but then her smooth brow furrowed. "Why couldn't he come here?"

Sybil spoke, "As your father said, he is too busy. He would not have time to entertain your uncle if he'd come. Let's not be sad, Helene. Let's enjoy this time together."

Mission control was a target too. Especially if the alien robots had extracted intel from *Concordia* or its personnel. Leclerc kept a confident smile on his face. Worried thoughts swirled behind them. He'd told Sybil to take Helene on vacation, to a cabin in the wooded hills near the border with Provence, far from anything aliens could want to destroy.

Sybil had refused. As far as they lived from mission control, if they were at risk at home, the aliens would have set the entire world on fire.

Leclerc leaned over the table, skewering fork in his left hand and carving knife in his right. The skin of the goose breast crackled as he carved it. He pinched a slice between the fork and knife and moved it to Helene's plate.

"Why haven't the aliens contacted us, Papa?" Disappointment ran through her voice.

Leclerc sucked in a breath. For months, he and Guo and everyone around mission control had told the world the aliens came in peace. Tension ran across his shoulders. He shared a long glance with Sybil. After a moment, she nodded.

"What is it?" Helene asked. "I can tell when you don't want me to know something."

Leclerc carved the rest of the goose breast and served it. All the while he fixed his posture to show Helene he would answer her soon. Finally, he sat and turned to her.

Helene's soft brown eyes, so much like her mother's, darted over his face. Her eyes moistened and her lower lip trembled. "It's not that they can't but that they won't? Then why did they come?"

He measured his words. "There is a chance they came with hostile intent."

"That's impossible," she blurted with the certainty of youth. "We have nothing they could want or need. The galaxy is more than big enough to share."

His mouth tightened. "Two centuries ago, by any logical measure, Europe was more than big enough to share. But you have gone on school field trips to Verdun. You have seen the ossuary at Douaumont."

She grimaced. Inwardly, he did too. Thick walls pierced by narrow windows, through which showed the bones and skulls of tens of thousands of men. Dead for no reason beyond the greed and vanity of foolish elites.

"But that was two centuries ago," Helene managed to say. "We know better. The aliens are a million years old! They must know a million times better!"

"Perhaps," he said. As the words left his mouth he knew his tone would aggravate her.

"You don't think it's only a chance, do you? You believe its a certainty they come to fight us." The fiery look in her eyes blended into sadness. "Why did you lie?"

"Because the aliens could pick up our broadcasts. We did not want to tip our hand." The poker metaphor made him briefly think of Memford and Aggarwal. He shoved the thought away. Those two had no place at his dinner table on Christmas Eve.

"We have defenses prepared," he explained. "If the aliens come in peace, the defenses will remain hidden and never used. If the aliens come in war, then we will use our defenses."

Helene dropped her fork and knife to her plate. She crossed her arms over her chest and slouched. A strand of her crimson hair fell in front of her eyes. "You're wrong."

"I hope so. Now, eat."

He didn't wait for her response. He knifed off a bite of his goose breast. In his mouth, the chestnut paste smoothed out the gamey flavor of the meat. He raised an eyebrow at Helene.

She huffed out a breath, then reached for her utensils.

Leclerc swallowed, then pierced green beans with his fork. Red words, brighter and bolder even than his daughter's dyed hair, filled the center of his vision.

Hostile activity. Targets struck in England and Bavaria. Defense force activated. Your presence required at mission control.

His hands froze.

Sybil noticed first. "What is it?"

"The aliens." Gently he set down his silverware. His shoulders rose before the rest of his body did. "I must go."

"They chose to attack on Christmas Eve?" She shook her head. "Apparently they did. I'll put together a plate for you."

"No need—"

"After the work I put in, I won't have you eat potato crisps from a vending machine." She stood, then reached for his plate. "I'll take care of it while you get ready to go."

"Thank you," he said. When she got close, he gave her a quick kissed.

Sybil bustled to the kitchen, leaving him alone with Helene. He turned to his daughter.

A strand of hair ran down her pallid cheek like fresh blood. Her lower lip quivered, until she snapped shut her mouth and angled her head down and away from him. "I bet you're happy."

"Only that we prepared a counterattack. Stay home. Don't over-react to any news coming through the media. They err at the best of times. I'll tell you the truth when I can."

She raised her head. Glowering, she said, "Not about the alien attack. If that's really what it is. You're happy you were right and I was wrong."

Her words made him fume, but he kept his emotions off his face and went to her. He leaned toward her, put his arm across her collar-bones in an embrace made awkward by the pointed finials on the rigid back of her chair and by her stiff shoulders.

"I wish you had been right," he said.

"You shouldn't have lied to me."

"If I don't at times lie to you, I'm not doing my job right."

"I don't want to hear about the agency—"

"No." He held her tighter. "My job as your father."

She leaned her head against the chair back. He could not see her eyes but from her posture he guessed she'd shut them in exasperation. "I'm not a child, Papa."

You'll always be my child, he thought but did not say. Instead he kissed the top of her dyed-crimson hair. "I forget sometimes."

She sniffed out a breath, but he sensed good humor in it. "Go do your work."

An hour later, he descended the broad stairs into the control room. An image of half of Earth filled the big board, compelled his eye.

Veiled by bands of cloud and storm, thick clusters of light marked the nighttime coasts of continents he could not identify. Farther inland, the lights thinned into scattered clumps of smaller cities. To the right, a sunlit tranche showed a cloud-dotted expanse of deep ocean.

Thick white lines arced around the globe. A pulsing red dot crawled along one of those lines. The alien ship. Coordinates, 26° north, 136° east. Somewhere over the western Pacific.

More red pulsed. Three Xs dotted a curve of urbanized coastline he suddenly realized was China. He couldn't tell which were in Traditionalist-controlled states versus Humanist ones. One more red X pulsed in Traditionalist Japan.

Only four? The ship's orbit would carry it well out of range of future strikes.

A pit opened in his gut. Out of range on this pass. In a few hours, it would be back over the Far East. After flying over thousands more cities and billions more people. Including his brother in Paris. Sybil and Helene not far from here.

At the horseshoe, Leclerc didn't recognize the two watch officers who'd drawn the swing shift on Christmas Eve. One Humanist, one Traditionalist, though God knew why the trans-factional redundancy mattered anymore. They hunched over their stations, alone except for the stuffed chimera and the toy alien on the ledge. The plastic ray gun in the alien's hand seemed in poor taste now.

"Mr. Leclerc." Guo's voice carried from behind him.

She stood at a workstation with the military personnel, incongruous amidst their buzz cuts and uniforms with her flowing black hair and a pullover sweater in a purplish shade Sybil would know the name of. Mauve or lilac. Her jade and porcelain yin-yang pendant lay tilted against her sweater's thick vertical ribs.

Leclerc went her way. His steps took him past the sitting area, now unoccupied and with its glass windows transparent. Someone had rearranged the black leather chairs and sofa, he idly noted. Ahead, the military men lost interest in him. Their gazes returned to their stations or the big board.

Guo also glanced at the giant video display. A thoughtful expression tightened her eyes, and lingered after she turned her gaze to him and he stopped walking. "A shame our guests were so rude they interrupted your family's Christmas Eve dinner."

He shrugged. "You had plans too, I should think?"

She shook her head enough to ripple the ends of her hair. "The alert came during a swim in the hotel's indoor pool. If the aliens had done nothing, I would right now be eating a room service dinner and catching up on paperwork."

"Alone?" He touched his fingertips to his forehead. Months of collaboration had forged something like a friendship, hadn't they? "I should have invited you to my house. We had more than enough food—"

"Your home is your sanctuary, to get away from work."

"For a few hours, it could have been yours as well."

She smiled at that. "Perhaps next year." She looked past him. "But for now...."

He craned his neck. A composite view of live satellite feeds, mapping data, and graphic overlays. Someone in the horseshoe had added wireframe borders to delineate continents and countries. Still just four red Xs in nighttime Japan and China, slipping toward the left limb of the Earth.

China.

Voice cautious, he said to Guo, "Are your family and friends safe?"

"Safe? I expect so. The strikes in China are no closer to them than Humanist headquarters in London, or the Traditionalist relay station in Bavaria, are to us here."

"One forgets how big a country or a nation can be."

"The strikes are extremely precise. The three targets in Chinese lands are the faction regional headquarters in Shanghai and Beijing, and your faction's spaceport in Uighurstan. They spared large civilian targets, infrastructure such as bridges, power plants, the Three Gorges Dam—"

A chill washed down Leclerc's torso. Billions of tons of water inundating city after city... "Wanton destruction is not their goal."

"Indeed. Their precise targeting happened not only in China, but in Europe and Russia as well. Also, the targets they did strike suffered minimal loss of life. Their blows landed here on late afternoon on Christmas Eve, and overnight in China and Japan."

Two columns of small video windows ran up the left side of the big board. One column showed live camera feeds of collapsed buildings, tongues of flame, firefighters and paramedics. The next column showed aerial composite images of nighttime neighborhoods, taken by helicopter or drone. One-to-one pairings. In the aerial views, the fires started by alien lasers glowed hot amid untouched neighborhoods.

"That could change on their subsequent passes," Leclerc said. "Hit command and control centers first, then strike broader targets later."

She gestured toward the uniformed men talking in low, clipped tones nearby. "Our military colleagues have advised civilian authorities worldwide to take civil defense measures." A faint smile touched her lips. "They have also prepared our counterattack."

He followed her gaze back to the view of Earth. In addition to the gray palette of city, cloud, and night, and the blood-red marks of the alien ship and the wounds it inflicted on the planet, two yellow dots appeared in the Pacific. Widely separated, one northeast of the alien ship and far into empty ocean, the other south of the Equator, only a thousand kilometers or so from Australia.

Arctic summer memories made him shiver. The submarines had come a long way from the drydock on the north coast of Russia.

They all had.

Behind them, one of the Russian naval officers spoke. "All submarines. You are hereby authorized to fire on alien ship."

25 DECEMBER 2132 (EARTH REFERENCE FRAME) | 26 FEBRUARY 2129 (*NAPOLEON* REFERENCE FRAME)

JAEGER FLOATED in the command room. The lights blazed at full power, but his body still ran on the ship's 24-hour clock. Just after oh-one-hundred. His eyes felt gritty. When his fingers brushed his jaw, a sandpaper sensation made him briefly wonder how long ago he'd last shaved. His right ankle gave him a low ache from hooking his foot in a grab strap for more hours than usual.

Near him, Ulanovas went from station to station, holding on with one hand and working the controls with the other. His eyes remained bright, watching the main display. "Perfect, okay?"

Jaeger squinted. Too many lights, too much information. "What's perfect?"

The Lithuanian sounded puzzled, as if it should be the most obvious thing in the room. "The hydrogen collector. Ah, it's not on screen. Here." He mashed buttons.

The main display jumped to a close up of Jupiter. The hydrogen collector looked intact.

"I don't see that we did anything."

"Infrared will show." He pressed more buttons. Browns and reds and yellows leached out of Jupiter's banded atmosphere, replaced with a grayscale cloudscape tinted blue.

Removing color from the images didn't change the appearance of the hydrogen collector station. Same gray cylinder. But now, a red plume jetted out from straight slash along its side. The plume spiraled from the cylinder's rotation.

"That red is the false color of the temperature of stored hydrogen," Jaeger said, not bothering to add a questioning inflection at the end.

"Exactly. The station is losing hydrogen. So much, the venting gas is like a rocket. The station's attitude control drives work extra hard to keep it in its orbit." He gestured in air. A telestrated oval surrounded blazing red pinpoints on the station's side, nearly opposite the hydrogen plume.

Outside the oval, the nav beacons on the near end of the station blinked in their usual pattern. "Crew compartment looks secure." Jaeger exhaled and tension left his shoulders. Human beings, safe. And available to rebuild the collector station and fuel up the next fleet of Bussard ramjets for a mission of vengeance to Alpha Centauri. After they safely returned to Brave Charlie.

"News is even better, okay? Look." Ulanovas paused the video. He wiped away the telestrated oval, then drew a new circle around a dull red pixel almost lost against the pallid blue of the false-colorized planet.

"Hydrogen. Not part of the plume." His sluggish mind dredged up the answer and made him blink. "We cut the umbilicus?"

"Exactly. This is a tiny amount of hydrogen leaking from the cut." Ulanovas's toothy grin shone in the bright lighting. "What hostile aliens would want to do. We cross the hydrogen collector off the list, okay?"

Jaeger nodded. "What's next?"

"We're over the Pacific Ocean now. Nothing to hit for the next thirty minutes but the Trad ground station in Samoa. I'll turn the lasers mostly onto the telescope array and other deep space targets. Targets in North America will come into range after that."

Jaeger rubbed his jaw to rouse himself. "All the ground targets have been clean hits so far?"

"I hit what I aimed at," Ulanovas said with an air of pretended annoyance at having his skills questioned.

Time to verify. Jaeger joined the public voice channel. "Annike, what news broadcasts have you seen and heard from Earth?"

She sounded upbeat despite the late hour. "The newsreaders talk of 'decapitation strikes'. They only speak of and show damage at targets on our list. They urge the masses to take shelter. Their overall tone is disbelieving and fearful. This is happening in broadcasts from both factions."

"Good," Jaeger said. "Fear now, anger late—"

An alarm sounded on one of the control stations. His sluggish head turned until he saw a flashing red light. "Extractor problem." He pulled himself closer, frown grooving his face.

Another red light flashed on. "Two extractors? One of them I overhauled last week. What's going on?"

Ulanovas pressed keys. Images cycled through the displays. Earth below, the sunlit Pacific Ocean gauzed over with clouds. A rear view, bits of drifting chaff glinting in sunlight.

As Jaeger watched the rear view, light flashed. More chaff burst into view, like someone flinging metallic confetti from offscreen.

From the back of the ship.

Another flash. More chaff, this one coming from another angle.

A third red light blinked on Jaeger's control panel.

His heart pounded. "They're shooting at us."

"Impossible," Ulanovas said.

On the life support panel, yellow and red LEDs kicked in. Hull breaches. "Then why the hell are we losing pressure near engineering?"

"The only thing below us is ocean, okay...." The Lithuanian's hand smacked his forehead, pushed back his sandy blond hair. "Weapons platforms on ships."

"Nuclear powered ones, I bet," said Jaeger. "To power a beam strong enough to punch through the hull." More light flashed on screen, but much less bright. A glancing blow, or a hit on the side of the ship?

"We must hit back."

McIlroy's voice came onto the public channel. "At what? Marie and I are looking at the visual feed and can't see any sign of a ship through the clouds."

Another flash of light. Another cloud of particles blown off the back. Jaeger rolled in his lips. His gaze darted to the control boards. Still only three blinking lights for damaged extractors. Some of the life support LEDs turned from red to yellow, or yellow to green. Automated systems walled off the hull breaches. But the gunners below had dialed in their weapons. "We need to take some evasive action. Turn the rock cap to face the surface."

"No," said Ulanovas. "Do that, and the forward weapons can't fire on the deep space telescope array, okay?"

"We can hit the telescope array on our way out of the system," Jaeger said. "Enough hits on the extractors and drives and we're sitting ducks!"

Over the public channel, McIlroy added, "We need time to find the targets if you want to shoot back."

"No. Must we? No?" Indecision sounded in Ulanovas's voice.

Another flash of light in the rear view. A fourth light started blinking. "That's a quarter of our extractors down!" Jaeger shouted. "Turn now!"

A second of garbled sounds, then Ulanovas found his voice. "Turning, nose down to Earth, in 3, 2, 1."

Jaeger's gut clenched. His gaze darted over the controls. Earth crept across the side view. Constellations and clouds of chaff trickled out of sight to the rear. Another flash, less bright. Any alloy particles burned off by this laser blast drifted off screen.

The count of blinking lights remained at four. A quarter of the ship's drives, damaged. Destroyed?

Ponderously, *Napoleon* continued its turn. Ulanovas switched to the forward view, through cameras deployed by robots on top of the rock cap. The planet came into sight. A laser flash turned some of the stone into a puff of dust.

Jaeger caught his breath. The rock cap protected the ship from interstellar gas and dust grains at relativistic speeds. It should shield them against lasers.

At least until they had to expose the back end of the ship to accelerate out of orbit.

Just before Jaeger pulled on the helmet of his pressure suit, Annike handed out stimulants. Caffeine and ginseng impregnated into a biopolymer film strip that dissolved on Jaeger's tongue and left a bitter aftertaste. Not a substitute for rest, but enough to keep him, and the others, going through the rest of *Napoleon*'s night.

She gave him a quick kiss before he sealed up his helmet. He pulled himself along the corridors to the engineering deck. His breath roared in his ears. The helmet wasn't required—he moved through air —but if some weakened bulkhead gave way as he passed....

He spiraled past empty decks like silent tombs until he came to a solid wall of alloy blocking his path.

"Marie? Mac?"

"Working on it," McIlroy said over the radio. From their station, with shirt sleeve temperatures and breathable air, they were supposed to be manipulating the alloy panels to flow into a makeshift airlock.

He hung in place, arms and legs jittery. He craned his neck. "What's taking so long?"

"You do not see it yet?" Marie asked.

"See wha—I do now."

In the spiraling rampway, glistening lines stretched from wall to wall and floor to ceiling. The lines rose, like the edges of knives pushed through the surfaces. Blade-thin sheets of alloy pushed toward the center of the rampway. Between them, a square of light shrank, shrank, disappeared.

His breath sounded ragged. The odor of fresh sweat clogged his nose.

"Check your suit," McIlroy said.

"Checking." Jaeger ran diagnostics. Telltales popped up on the inside of his visor. Green lights. The external pressure gauge read fifteen PSI around him, twelve inside his suit. "All clear."

McIlroy spoke. "Opening to breach zone now."

Jaeger turned. The solid wall of alloy between him and the engineering deck looked like a reversed video of what he'd just seen. A square hole formed in the middle of the wall, and widened. A puff of flash-frozen humidity steamed through the hole away from him. The external gauge dropped to zero long before the wall receded into the surfaces of the rampway.

"Going through."

He moved from handhold to handhold until he came to the corridor ringing the engineering deck. At first, it looked normal. Most of the lights remained on. Only the pressure gauge gave any hint of something amiss.

But soon he found evidence of laser impacts. Clouds of metal flakes drifted in the airless corridor. He wriggled past them, wary of sharp edges. Status boards flashed in lunatic error patterns. He opened an accessway to find another cloud of metal fragments.

From his external tool kit, he pulled off a mirror on a telescoping rod. The hook-and-loop fabric resisted his hand, but gave way without a sound.

He extended the mirror and adjusted its angle until he saw something he at first couldn't recognize. He had to blink to see it for what it was. A borehole as big around as his forearm, its walls glowing a dull red when he called up an infrared overlay. At the far end of the bore-hole showed a blackness dotted with glittering stars.

A chill formed in his gut. The incoming beam had pierced five meters of alloy. A massive amount of power had driven it. Who'd engineered the laser weapon? Humanists? Traditionalists? Both?

You wanted them to work together against an alien threat, didn't you?

Jaeger took a few breaths to calm himself, then used an inclinometer to measure the beam's incident angle. Send the data upstairs. Then move to the next downed extractor....

Two hours later, he left engineering. Marie reversed the steps of the improvised airlock. When the square between Jaeger and the main space of the ship dilated and the pressure gauge climbed, he longed to pull off the helmet. He resisted until he was back at the inhabited deck, where he found everyone else clustered around the entrance to the control room.

Annike came toward him. Her graceful hands took his helmet. Her brown eyes studied him. "How bad is it?" she asked. From her tone, she expected it to be bad indeed.

"Four extractors down. Hard. Maybe I can repair them, but it would take days for each." The faces around him looked glum. "I'm not the only one with bad news, am I?"

From inside the control room, Ulanovas's voice sounded defensive. "We scored some hits in North America. Humanist headquarters in Silicon Valley. Launch command at Canaveral."

"Both unstaffed on Christmas Day," said Annike.

Some good news, at least. Jaeger drew in a breath. "What about the laser ships?"

McIlroy scratched at his beard. "Not ships. Submarines."

"Submarines. How'd you figure that out?"

"We took the incident angle data you sent us from all the impacts, then pinpointed the beam origins to two locations in the Pacific Ocean. We're back over that part of Earth and looking for surface ships big enough to generate the required power. None within two hundred kilometers of either site. And no aircraft can carry a power plant big enough to do the job."

Ulanovas sounded testy. "Submarines cannot go fast when submerged, okay? We can fire in vicinity."

"I reckon all we'd do is boil a few tons of seawater." McIlroy raised his voice and aimed it into the control room. "Not worth it."

"And there are more submarines," Marie said to Jaeger. "We took fire over the Atlantic. Luckily it only hit the rock cap."

The bitter taste of the stimulant strip came back to Jaeger. He rubbed his eyes. "Lucky or not, each hit on the rack cap will punch a five-meter hole in it. Enough hits, and it could lose integrity. If it falls apart during the boost phase back to Alpha Centauri, we're dead."

Ulanovas came to the control room door. His eyes challenged Jaeger. "You want to run?" he asked.

"Our first goal was to unify Earth. We've done that. Our second goal was to damage Earth's interstellar infrastructure enough for us to get back to Bravo Charlie before they can catch us. We've done that too. Time to go."

Hands on hips, elbows jutting out, Ulanovas said, "Aliens would not show weakness."

"Aliens would retreat before they risked their own lives," McIlroy said.

Ulanovas shook his head. "There are more targets to hit."

"We don't need to hit more on Earth," Jaeger replied. "The ones in deep space, telescopes of the array, we can hit as we boost out."

"We boost out, we expose the back of the ship. May lose more extractors." Ulanovas's gaze went to each of them, hoping someone would take his side.

McIlroy jutted his chin at the Lithuanian. "We have to boost out sometime."

"We knock out submarines first—"

"How are we going to find the submarines," McIlroy said, exaggerating a Texas drawl, "never mind damage them?"

Ulanovas's hands slid along his legs. He hung his head. "You make good points, okay?"

Jaeger spoke. "We depart when we're less exposed to submarines. Somewhere over central Asia would be our best bet."

"That's an hour from now?" Annike said.

"Give or take."

Her brown eyes went from Jaeger to Ulanovas. "Can we be ready by then?"

Ulanovas met her gaze. "An hour is more than enough time, for me."

Jaeger smiled. If you needed the Lithuanian to do something, just doubt his ability to do it. "I might need another orbit to do pre-flight checks on the remaining extractors."

"Don't keep us here too long," Ulanovas said. He interdigitated his hands, turned them around, cracked his knuckles.

Could the factions have mounted laser systems on trains or fleets of tractor-trailers? Jaeger kept his smile on his face.

No, he decided. Ground-based weapons platforms would be much easier to see from orbit. Much easier to hit.

But putting them in the middle of continents would fill gaps in the defenses....

Jaeger rubbed his eyes. Get *Napoleon* ready to depart. Pick the safest time window to boost out of orbit.

He'd unified Earth against an alien threat. Time for the people on the ground to take the next steps.

CHAPTER 19

25 DECEMBER 2132

The big board showed the alien ship orbited high above central Asia. A window in the upper right corner showed a live telephoto feed from a chase plane sent up by the Russian air force. The stabilizing algorithm in the live feed gained and lost focus, like someone fumbling with a pair of binoculars. Even when the alien ship came into focus, grains of dust and metal shimmered around its rocky cap facing Earth.

Leclerc leaned his elbow on the horseshoe ledge. The toy alien lay on its back, blaster aimed at the distant ceiling, like a chess king toppled over in mate. Despite the late hour, warmth ran through his gut and his thoughts danced.

They'd damaged the enemy ship. Fired at it from every angle. Forced it to shield itself with the rocky cap, as if the joint defense force's laser weapons were as dangerous as a relativistic passage through interstellar space. The aliens still fired, true, but with the same precision at empty buildings and repairable infrastructure.

An odd way to neutralize a rival species that had just taken its first steps into the galaxy.

Perhaps the alien robots did think in some truly strange manner. Or their masters had programmed into them some ethical qualms or religious beliefs that stopped them from devastating the planet.

Or....

He shook his head. More tired than he thought.

Something moved in the chase plane view. Adrenaline surged through him.

The alien ship pivoted.

"What's it doing?" he wondered aloud.

Silence from the technicians crewing the horseshoe. A distant bustle of low conversations and brisk activity from the military men in the back. Near him, Guo spoke. "Perhaps they are preparing to retreat."

"Or they're going to stage two. Flip one-eighty and use the drives to lance their way across central Asia and the Far East." After he spoke, the ramifications of his words sunk in. Not targeted strikes on spaceports and faction headquarters, far from Guo's friends and family. Swathes of destruction across Chinese cities, Humanist and Traditionalist alike.

His head snapped around. Nervous fingers dabbed at his cropped crown of hair.

Guo, however, merely watched the turning ship with a ghost of a smile. "I do not think they plan such a thing, Mr. Leclerc."

"How can you tell?"

She raised a finger. "We'll talk about it soon, but not now."

The ship stopped turning. Leclerc let out a sigh. Though blurrier now, after a ninety degree turn, the rear of the ship dominated the view. The rock cap faced left and the sixteen drives faced right. Only the weapons emplacements on the ship's cylindrical flank could harm any targets on the surface. The beam path of the drives ran on a harm-less tangent away from the curve of Earth.

A clipped American voice boomed from the loudspeakers. "Attention all submarines in Atlantic, Arctic, Mediterranean, Arabian Sea. The alien ship has exposed its rear to the west. You are authorized to fire if you have line-of-sight." A pause, then the American repeated, "Attention all sub—"

One of the other military personnel must have flicked a switch that cut off the American from the speakers.

In the window, the algorithm fought to focus. The alien ship had to be far downrange of the chase plane now, and receding another seven klicks every second. Any moment now, it could fire its drives and leave orbit—

A flash of light. A shower of metal fragments erupted from the rear.

Another.

Another—

Light blazed from the rear ship. Leclerc squinted, until the display desaturated the glow and his eyes adjusted. On the ground in central Asia, it would look like the sun had leaped into the sky.

The blazing light could well show from the parking lot outside. From the windows of his house, where Sybil probably lay awake, too anxious to sleep.

"Alien ship is leaving orbit," said someone behind him in the horseshoe.

Another voice, speeding up and growing louder as it said, "Acceleration about 7.4 m/s^2. On a heading to Alpha Centauri. They're retreating!"

Cheers echoed off hard surfaces and double-height walls. Civilians jumped up and down and hugged one another.

When was the last time the cavernous room felt so warm, its personnel so united? When data came showing *Concordia*'s arrival at Bravo Charlie, a year and a half ago? No, not even then.

Leclerc watched the alien ship's slow retreat. The display

dimmed far enough to separate the individual shafts of actinic light emerging from ten drives.

Ten? He counted again. Six dark spots dotted the ring of lights.

A military voice, unamplified, boomed from their workstation in the back. "Keep firing!"

Light flashed on the alien ship's flank. More alloy flaked off. The ship accelerated past the particle cloud. The intense beams from the drives vaporized the flakes in an instant.

A shudder ran over Leclerc's shoulders and down his chest, dissonant against the ebullient mood filling mission control. The alien ship could have destroyed cities and killed billions, and the joint defense submarines could not have stopped it.

He leaned toward Guo. "We are very lucky," he muttered.

She turned her head far enough to raise an eyebrow. "I doubt it is luck."

The alien ship tweaked its heading as it continued its ponderous departure. The chase plane view flickered, replaced with a sharper one from a steep angle catching mostly the rock cap. A chase plane from the Ganges Republic air force, high over the Himalayas.

It took Leclerc a moment to remember that the Ganges Republic was a Traditionalist state. How little the factions meant now.

"Acceleration down! Now 6.8 m/s^2!"

Down but not done. The big board projected the ship's current vector, heading southeast on a climb over Thailand and Indonesia. In his mind, Leclerc drew a cone backward, from the ship's drives over the bulk of Asia. No submarines there. Even though the ship would soon pass over shallower waters off southeast Asia, the submarines only sailed in deep ocean, to maximize their ability to evade alien fire.

Potshots, perhaps, but little chance of further damage.

Over the next hour, the mood in the room remained upbeat. One of the people in the horseshoe propped up the stuffed chimera. It stood over the fallen alien like an angry boxer. Even the military personnel relaxed after the ship climbed past the altitude of geosynchronous orbit and kept accelerating. The lancing beams of its drives knocked out a comm sat, but stayed well clear of Earth.

A final vector adjustment aimed the alien ship toward Alpha Centauri.

"Can it truly be gone?" Leclerc mused.

Guo nodded at the big board. "It appears so." She turned to him. The overhead lights glossed in her black hair, and she looked far too chipper for the late hour. "We should draft a public announcement, to deliver in the morning."

He stretched his arms over his head. "We can find an empty office somewhere in the building."

She extended a hand toward the transparent glass walls of the sitting area. "Would there do?"

"Of course." He gestured for her to lead.

In the sitting area, the couch and two chairs stood at a ninety degree angle to each other, accentuating the straight lines of black leather and steel. The chessboard in the glass box occasional table held the same game position, the pieces of shells and casings poised for a devastating exchange. An exchange that would never take place, the game declared a draw by mutual agreement.

He followed her in and shut the door behind him.

"Lock it, please," Guo said. She waved a finger in the air. Gray frosted the walls. By the time he reached the chair nearest her spot on the couch, the walls had fully opaqued. Only the constant stream of data projected into his eyes by the display driver in his wearable connected him with the outside world.

Leclerc gave Guo an appraising look. "You don't want to draft an announcement, do you?"

"We'll get to that," she said. Lights in the sitting area's ceiling of glass cast down spots glinting on the porcelain and jade of her pendant. Yin and yang, cosmic balance.

With precise movements of her fingers, she lifted the pendant from around her neck. She pressed her knees together and dropped it in her lap. Links of the pendant's chain slithered as it fell.

One-handed, she unzipped a hidden pocket in her sweater and pulled out a piece of fabric. A sheen like oil ran through the fabric as she unfolded it into a sack more than big enough to hold the pendant. She slid the pendant in and shook the sack to settle the coiled chain inside.

"Your wearable, please."

Leclerc studied her face. The wisp of a smile he'd glimpsed throughout the night had come back.

A moment's hesitation, then trust flooded him. He reached into his shirt and drew out his wearable. Its lanyard hung up on the tip of his nose before he pulled it free.

He handed it to her. She dropped it in the sack and zipped the sack closed. As the pull joined the last few teeth, the streams of data in his eyes winked out.

An RF—blocking fabric made up the sack. Inside the grayed glass walls, they were as alone as a space crew orbiting the far side of the moon.

"What do you wish to talk about?" he asked.

She turned to the glass box. Her fingers found a magnetic clasp and pushed. The top of the box, hinged on the side away from her, popped up. "While we've been here tonight—this morning?—I've thought back on our conversation in California." She put the sack with their wearables on an empty square, like a third force had landed a queen to disrupt the unwinnable game.

He waited until Guo lowered and reclasped the lid. "About the alien ship and its motives," he said.

"We agreed biological aliens could not have survived, even in suspended animation, for a million years. We concluded their ship is robotic, acting on programming given it by extinct masters. Inexplicable programming. Wait until an intelligent civilization comes to you, then attack that civilization's nearest world? And attack, with precision, political targets only?"

"The alien ship damaged the hydrogen collector in Jupiter orbit," he reminded her.

"Damaged, but not destroyed. Preliminary reports suggest it can be repaired. And the crew compartment was untouched."

"They hit spaceports on Earth. Canaveral. Baikonur—"

"Again, damaged, but not destroyed. And with their skilled workers home for the evening or the holiday."

Leclerc rolled his wrists in a shrug. "Robots with inexplicable programming. There's no other explanation."

"Is there?" She glanced at the sack with their wearables. "In fact, there are six."

Six? "Perhaps it is the late hour," he said. "I don't follow."

"Six of *Concordia*'s personnel were rated for xenology, against the chance primitive or extinct intelligent life lived on Bravo Charlie. Jaeger, d'Arbaud, and Ulanovas from the Traditionalist side. McIlroy, Feng, and Ingvarsson from yours."

"I don't recall the names."

"I refreshed myself on the facts a few weeks ago," said Guo. "We know *Concordia* sent down a surface expedition, to a site not far from the alien ship's hiding place and launch point."

"You think they might be flying the alien ship? Absurd."

Guo arched an eyebrow in reply.

"An alien ship would be such a prize for mankind," Leclerc said, "they would have flown it home and announced themselves to a hero's welcome."

"Flown it home, and delivered it to which faction?"

"The knowledge gained by *Concordia* is to be shared between them." Or should he say? "Us."

"From what I know of the highest ranks in St. Petersburg, the inner party would gladly share knowledge about the rocks and plants and non-sapient animals of Bravo Charlie. Would the same hold for the Humanist leadership?"

Neville, Rubik, even Memford? "Yes."

"The alien ship has a propulsion system centuries more advanced than *Concordia*'s. A propulsion system of immense power. The Traditionalist inner party would plot to seize it for themselves."

"The same would hold for London."

"If not seized, that power would be developed by both factions," Guo said. Leclerc opened his mouth to speak and she jutted up a finger to cut him off. "Like hydrogen bombs in the twentieth century or nanotechnological plagues in the twenty-first. Except the power of the alien ship would be so much greater, that if weaponized, it could cause an extinction event."

A chill lifted the stubble over Leclerc's neck and jaw. "The aliens had factions too."

"If the alien survivors on Bravo Charlie could leave a decipherable message for our personnel to fly their ship, could they also leave a decipherable message about the cause of their homeworld's destruction?"

"A reasonable assumption."

"Another reasonable assumption is that our personnel could see the parallels between the alien homeworld's fate and the cold war between our factions in the half century since Wáng's defeat."

"I follow what you're saying, but why...." He waved at the glass panel of gray behind him, in the direction of the big board. His hand dropped. "To bring about peace between our factions, they pretended to be Wáng."

"Or Wilhelm II, or Napoleon, or...." Guo's smile deepened. "You see my point."

"Unite them against a common enemy." Leclerc considered. "Which explains their targeting. Both factions hit in equal measure. Political targets to scare the faction leaders into collaborating. Space infrastructure damaged but not destroyed. An attack that looks more hostile than it is."

His eyes went wide. Months of collaboration to defend Earth from an alien threat. But if it wasn't, would that collaboration disappear, and the cold war return? He studied her face, looking for some clue of her intentions. "Are you going to tell your superiors that the alien attack was a hoax?"

"No more than you will, I should think."

He nodded. She'd judged him correctly, to take him into her confidence. Thoughts pooled inside him and he gave a little shrug. "We have no real secret to keep. We are merely speculating between ourselves, after all. We have no evidence against the idea we were attacked by hostile alien intelligences."

Guo inclined her head, expressing disagreement tinged with a faint smile. "We have no evidence *yet*."

A warm feeling expanded Leclerc's chest. "Not until a joint expedition follows the ship back to Alpha Centauri."

I'm **RAYMUND EICH.** I use my Middle American upbringing as a launchpad for journeys to the ends of the Universe.

Growing up in the Midwest prepared me for my academic career, culminating with a Ph.D. in biochemistry from Rice University. It helps me help inventors prosper from their progress in medicine, biotechnology, and computer hardware.

Above all, it inspires me to write science fiction and fantasy about ordinary people facing extraordinary wonders and horrors, battling enemies both foreign and domestic, and building better lives for themselves, their families, and their societies.

My last name has one syllable and is pronounced "eye-sh." I live in Houston with my family.

Connect with me at **www.raymundeich.com** or follow the QR code below.

Online and brick-and-mortar bookstores around the world list millions of books, with thousands more published every day. I'm glad you discovered this one.

If you'd like to know when I release a new book, instead of leaving it to chance, join my Readers Club. I'll email you every two months with publishing news, an off-beat patent, and a short personal update. Plus, I'll let you know about an older book of mine you might have missed.

Yes, please! I'll go to **www.raymundeich.com/mailing-list** or scan the QR code below.

No thanks. I'll take my chances next time I look for your books.

Available wherever books are sold.

Learn more about these titles at our website, **www.cv2books.com,** or follow the QR code below.

Concordia's mission reflected the best of the human race. Crew and scientists from both of Earth's rival factions, Humanists and Traditionalists, journeyed for years at relativistic speeds to reach Bravo Charlie, a life-bearing planet orbiting Alpha Centauri B, to expand the frontiers of knowledge for all.

Concordia's mission also reflected humanity at its worst. Corrupt bureaucrats and ambitious political leaders in both factions maintained a status quo backed by weapons of mass destruction. The faction commanders on the mission each sought to seize advantages for their side alone.

Then the ship received transmissions. Signs of an ancient, powerful alien presence on the planet below.

Exploration 2127

Sent to explore, **Jaeger** and **McIlroy**, born and raised in a Texas divided by razor wire and minefields. Men torn between the mission's ideals and orders from their respective faction commanders, oily Varanathan and domineering Sandford.

Then Jaeger and McIlroy discover how to bring Earth's factions together... using knowledge given by aliens dead over a million years.

Earth barely survived the 21st Century.

Biotechnological and nuclear terrorism, civil war, famine, and ethnic cleansing killed billions. Thousands fled on warpdrive ships to colonize planets around distant suns.

In the 22nd century, after Earth unified under one world government, it opened wormhole links to the distant colonies, to prevent a repeat of the previous century's chaos on a galactic scale.

Enter operative Stone Chalmers. Spy. Assassin. Instrument maintaining Earth's dominion over all human worlds.

Opposing him are hostile forces on colony worlds... and within the Earth government itself.

When Stone clashes with those forces, Earth—and every human world—will be transformed forever.

Learn more about the Stone Chalmers series at
www.cv2books.com/stone-chalmers, or follow the QR code below.

The Progress of Mankind

To maintain order in the 22nd century, Earth relocates undesirables through artificial wormholes onto colony planets. Everyone benefits... except the planets' original colonists.

Now, the newly rediscovered colony of New Moravia learns Earth's plan and fights back.

The Greater Glory of God

Thousands fled the chaos of the 21st century on rogue warpdrive ships to settle colony planets. When Earth reunified in the 22nd, its fleets rediscovered the colonies and hunted down the warpdrive ships.

Every warpdrive ship but one.

To All High Emprise Consecrated

Unified Earth has rediscovered the colony of Minerva. Prosperous and technologically advanced, Minerva quickly submits to Earth supremacy.

Surprisingly quickly...

In Public Convocation Assembled

Earth's government controls all human colonies scattered through the galaxy by means of wormholes, warpdrive ships, and ruthless operatives. Operatives working to strengthen Earth's grip.

Or destroy it.

Take the Shilling

The Confederated Worlds implanted in his brain the skills to make him a soldier. Tomas Neumann had to learn for himself how to survive interstellar war.

Operation Iago

The Confederated Worlds lost the war. Can Lt. Tomas Neumann win the peace against elusive, deceptive foes out to turn the Confederated Worlds against itself?

A Bodyguard of Lies

Assigned to the halls of power, only Capt. Tomas Neumann can save the Confederated Worlds from the ultimate treachery.

The Blank Slate

Neuroscience entrepreneur Clay Shieffer must stop a tyrannical president... because he unwittingly gave the tyrant power over the human mind.

New California

After New California's founder committed suicide, two men vied to rule the colony.

Ashwin George, supported by the colony's elite and the Chinese company dominating half the settled galaxy.

Against him, Desmond Park, nanotechnology engineer, armed with the most formidable weapon of all.

A single idea.

The Reincarnation Run

Skeptical spacejock Landry Krieger knows exactly how to smuggle the "reborn" spiritual leader of an oppressed people past their conquerors... but the boy's priests—and governess—shake up his orderly plans.

Azureseas: Cantrell's War

Ross Cantrell joined the animal control mission on the newly-discovered planet Azureseas to earn the money to start married life together with his girlfriend.

Then Ross discovers the truth about the planet's "animals."

The ALECS Quartet

He had a month to learn the planet's mysteries—and Juliette's.

His cover story: return to Elard to dismantle his sect's missionary work to the planet's natives.

His true mission: investigate decades-old mysteries of love and death.

His objective: return to Earth with his discovery.

If he can.

A Mighty Fortress

Theodore and his team from the Lutheran Interstellar Terraforming Society would transform a barren, rocky world into a refuge of faith and life.

Or die trying.

Winner and the Poacher

A Portia Oakeshott, Dinosaur Veterinarian Short Novel

As a consultant to law enforcement, Portia confronts stark evidence of a rich young man's crime: the mounted head of a massive herbivorous *Wintonotitan*. A winner.

A dinosaur the company never granted a permit for hunting.

The First Voyages: The Complete Science Fiction Stories 1998-2012

From 21st century asteroid settlements to World War II Romania, from an Earth dominated by immortal aliens to Christ's empty tomb, a fresh, distinctive voice in science fiction will take you on journeys to the photosphere of the sun, the coding regions of DNA, and the complexities of the human psyche.

Stage Separations: The Complete Science Fiction Stories 2013-2018

In these pages, you can...

...race against time to solve mysteries hidden in a planet's vast desert—and in a woman's heart

...learn the true story of a president's assassination

...journey 14,000 miles to a high-tech fountain of youth

...win or go "home"—to an Earth you've never seen

and explore six other worlds created by a distinctive voice in twenty-first century science fiction.

Orbital Maneuvers: The Complete Science Fiction Stories 2019-2020

In these pages, you can join–

A mission to terraform a lifeless, rocky planet | A private detective uncovering the ultimate crime | A woman called by an ex-boyfriend... who's been dead twenty years | A President breaking his country's highest law | A star athlete discovering the true price of a championship

–and enjoy five more tales, in the latest installment of the Complete Science Fiction Stories of Raymund Eich.